MW01615978

FLOODWATERS

ADAM GNADE

Praise for *Float Me Away, Floodwaters*

"Gnade is the king of underground fiction. Every word is truth." —Nathaniel Kennon Perkins, author of *Wallop* and *The Way Cities Feel to Us Now*

"This book reads like a prayer that we can all somehow stay afloat in this country deluged with sadness and pain." —Bart Schaneman, author of *The Silence is the Noise* and *Someplace Else*

"An incantation for the end times." —Julia Eff, author of *Don't Piss Down My Back & Tell Me It's Raining*

"Part ghost story, part hymnal, and part adventure guide, Gnade's latest thrums with wonder, and dread, and bloody, exhilarating life." —Erik Henriksen, WIRED, Tor.com, and StarTrek.com contributor, author of *The Un-Inventor*

"The quiet poetry in Adam's fiction finds me like a treasured junk in the junk lot." —Rich Biaocco, author of *Death in a Rifle Garden* and *Torch Ballads*

"When the wheels are moving under you, in those quiet moments between destinations, *Float Me Away, Floodwaters* speaks volumes." —Nick Bernal, Burn All Books

"This is Gnade doing what he does best: pack practically every page with stark emotion, reflection, and insight. Though it is one of his shorter works, he still manages to create a very vivid, textured place that you'll want to live in for a while." —Jonas Cannon, author of *Cheer the Eff Up*

"*Float Me Away, Floodwaters* shows us snapshots of the real America—wild and lonesome, ugly-beautiful—it's Adam Gnade's best work yet." —Jessie Lynn McMains, author of *The Loneliest Show on Earth* and *Wisconsin Death Trip*

Float Me Away, Floodwaters

A pocketsize novel concerning modern farm living,
wayward country punks, and the New Old West

Adam Gnade

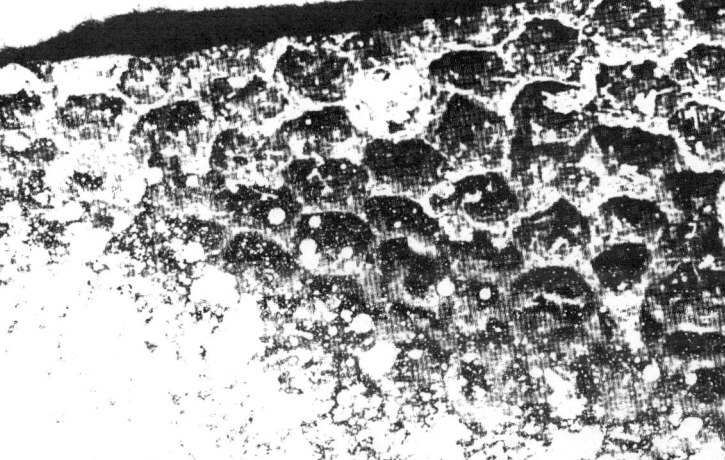

PUBLISHED IN COLLABORATION BY
BREAD AND ROSES PRESS AND THREE ONE G

Three One G, PO Box 178262, San Diego, CA 92117
Bread and Roses Press, PO Box 410, Chelsea, MI 48118

Float Me Away, Floodwaters / by Adam Gnade

Bread and Roses Press / Three One G, first printing
January 2021

Cover, book design, hand lettering / by Bran Black Moon

Photos / by Reira Rose Moon & Bran Black Moon

ISBN 978-1-939899-37-8

Copyright 2021 by Bread and Roses Press / Three One G

This book is a work of fiction.

PRINTED IN THE UNITED STATES OF AMERICA

1 3 5 7 9 10 8 6 4 2

ALSO BY ADAM GNADE

Fiction

Hymn California
Caveworld
Locust House
This is the End of Something But It's Not the End of You

Non-fiction

The Do-It-Yourself Guide to Fighting the Big
Motherfuckin' Sad

"For I would ride with you upon the wind."
-W.B. Yeats

"Time, she's a fast old train/She's here and then she's
gone/and she won't come again"
-Townes Van Zandt

Float Me Away, Floodwaters

PART

ONE

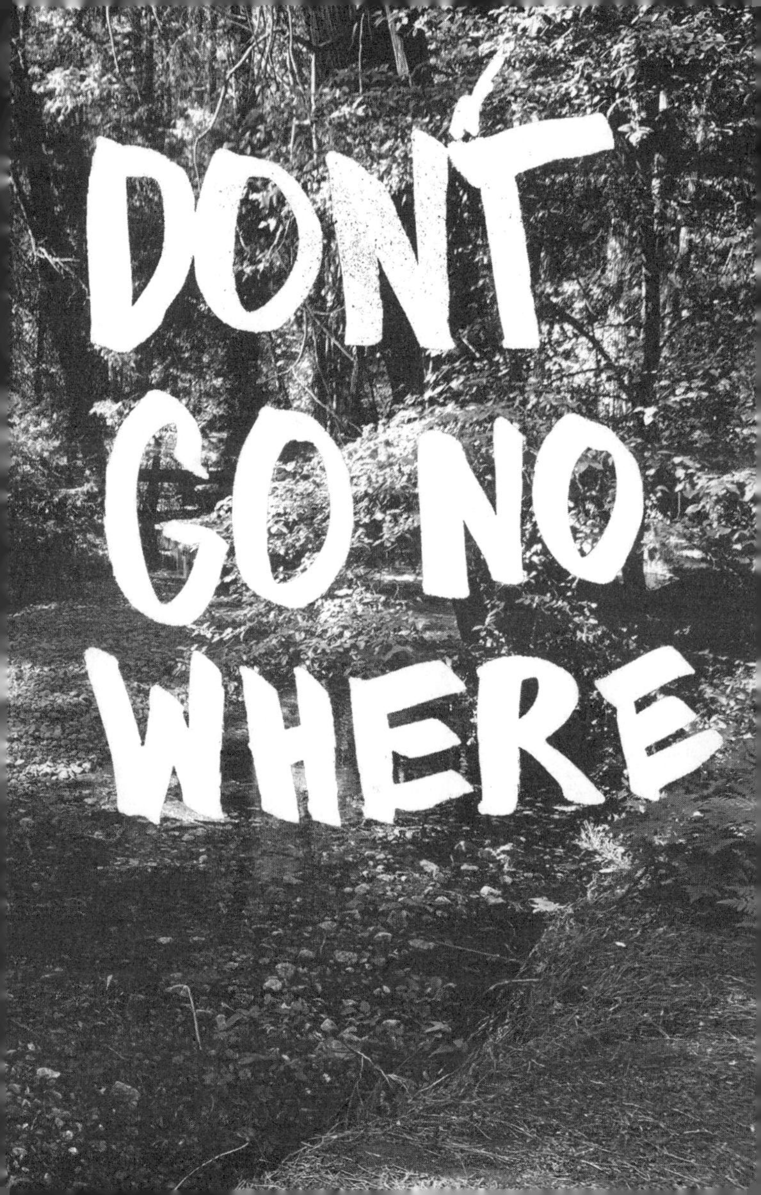
DON'T
GO NO
WHERE

Summer, 2018

1 • There's a man fishing under the train bridge. He stands on the rocks a few feet from the shaded water, casting out his line—the line and bait and sinker arcing gracefully in the air, the sun catching the line, and for a moment it shines like a strand of polished glass.

2 • You can smell the river park's lawn. It's fresh cut—a summer smell. You can smell the gas from the mower. It's barely there, on the breeze—a prickling tang in your nostrils along with hotdogs grilling and vanilla Swisher Sweets and coconut suntan lotion from the people on towels laying out.

3 • As you get closer it's the smell of the river—earthy, a desert kind of earthy next to the woody scent of the reeds and cattails. Underneath that it's the smell of mud and wet rock.

4 • As you near the shore it's the smell of hot sand. It's a mineral smell, salty, a smell like diamonds if diamonds had a smell—a beach scent without the sea.

5 • I drop my rolled-up towel on the sand at the riverbank, pull my t-shirt over my head, and kick off my sneakers. I haven't slept in two days. It might be three. After the first day and a half awake the details matter less and less.

6 • Under the train bridge I wade out into the water of the Colorado River—a mild and shallow stretch of it running

through the northern edge of Yuma, Arizona, the blonde sand sinking beneath my feet, thick grains, coarse like bits of gravel between your toes but finer the deeper you go. The water is warm. The smell of desert and sage and dry grass sharp in the air. In the shade under the overpass I sit cross-legged, the water up to my neck, and it moves around me and I dunk my head back and wash off the sweat of the past few days. It's good to be clean. I feel alive, fresh, quiet inside, steady. I smile up at the overpass because I'm exhausted and because the train tracks are beautiful with the rectangular spaces of bright blue sky shining through them and I think of how I would explain it to Alison (the dark metal and wood, the wood that smells of tar even from this distance). There's maybe a dozen of us in the water under the overpass. Sketchy dudes shirtless with silver cans of beer. An old man with a long gray mullet off on the edge of the group, standing waist deep, hands on his narrow hips, staring off downriver. Couples. Boys with shaved heads or rattails. Teenage girls in swimsuits and crop tops. Everyone floating off on their own or in small groups and then—

7 • —the train.

8 • —the train passing overhead from out of nowhere and all the sounds in the universe are blotted out to a crashing CHING CHING CHING CHING CHING—

9 • —and you feel it inside your chest, in your guts, in the marrow of your bones. I shut my eyes and hear nothing but the train and feel nothing but the warm water moving and the

sand below my crossed legs.

10 • After the train has passed, specks of dust drift down from the bridge above us. The dust hangs in the gauzy light—silent, burnished like hot copper, dark and golden.

11 • And then in the silence I hear myself think: *But you will DIE someday. At some point you won't exist and time will go on forever without you.* I don't want to tell myself this, but it comes on its own.

12 • I shut my eyes again and push it away. *No. Fuck you. Don't ruin this.*

13 • When I open my eyes, the dust is gone. I dig my hands into the wet sand below me looking for what I don't know and then—

14 • —and then a slurry, drawling voice behind me says, "Ey man you gahha light?"

15 • I swim-turn around and it's a guy my age wading toward me. He's skinny to the point of it being a problem and he's got the words "Country Fucking Music" tattooed as an arch across his chest in Old English script. When he gets close he lets himself sink to his shoulders just like I am then sticks an arm

out of the water. It splashes me and the splash startles me. My nerves are shot to hell, but I take his hand and shake it. "Man, you awright?" "Huh? Am I—" "I axed if you had a *light* and you just looked at me like I got *spaghetti* for hair." He laughs as I try to remember the question. "I don't rem— *Oh*. Right. Yeah, no, sorry I don't have a light. I *mean*—" I realize then it's been a few days since I've said anything out loud. Not since Austin. He stares up at the tracks above us, squinting, and then he says, "Yeah, man, I guess. We *all* wet here. Ain nobody gahha light." "Sorry ... that I don't." "Nobody *does*, man. Thas just how it *is*." He shakes his head. He's wearing an old red corduroy trucker cap that reads "Lakeside Speedway" in tilted white and blue lettering that's meant to give the impression of fast movement, and now I notice tattoos, tiny ones along his jawline and across his cheekbones. Text. Words. Too small for me to read. "*Ey*, I'm Lakeside Speed Wayne," he says, sticking his skinny arm out of the water again. I shake his hand for the second time. "James," I say. "James who? James and the fuckin' Giant fuckin' Peach?" he laughs, and then I'm laughing too. Maybe I'm laughing because I haven't slept, but that doesn't matter, I'm laughing regardless and it feels great. It feels like all is right with the world, like we will never die, none of us, we will keep on driving through faded desert towns, keep staying awake for days, keep wading out into calm rivers, keep meeting new people, keep shaking hands over and over again, keep laughing, keep asking questions just to maybe ask questions. "James Jackson Bozic," I say. "Sweet, man. Cool name. 'S good to meet you. This place, man. This. Fucking. Plaaace."

16 • "Yeah, this place," I nod.

17 • "This ... *plaaaaaace*," he drawls quietly, staring up at the bridge and the tracks above us.

18 • We sit in silence for a while.

19 • I dig into the sand and find a pebble then sidearm it across the surface of the water. It skips once and then it's gone. "Naw, man, watch this. See a true champion at work," he says, and his arm jerks out from the water and a black flash leaves his hand in a whipping snap. The rock skips once, once more, three times, a fourth, a triumphant fifth, and an extravagant *sixth* before it flicks through the cattails like a bullet. "Lakeside Speed Waaaayne!" he shouts, arms raised out of the water above his head. "Woop woop! Yeeeeah! Come meet the champion, muhfuckers!"

20 • Two of our fellow swimmers turn to look. The rest ignore us. It's quiet again.

21 • I hear a girl laugh behind me.

22 • A beer can snaps open.

23 • Someone sneezes and someone god blesses them. Someone says, softly, quietly, "Bro, I would freakin' *kill* for a pizza right now."

24 • A guy and a girl stand up from the water and wade to shore, holding hands, tall, slim, dark-skinned, faces close, talking soundlessly. "Lovebirds," says Lakeside Speed Wayne matter-of-factly, jutting his chin at them.

25 • I nod at his red trucker cap and say, "Your Lakeside Speedway hat ... we've got a track called Lakeside Speedway where I live. Just outside Leavenworth. In Kansas." "My maaan!" his arm sticks out of the water again and we shake hands for the third time. "My my my my *man*! You'll never believe this but I lived in Lev'worth all my *life* 'fore I came out here. Muhfuckers called me Lakeside Speed Wayne 'cause I'm Wayne—" he lays a hand on his chest and bows his head "—and I worked at the track sellin' nachos since I was a *baby*. You ever go?" "Yeah, totally. I was just there, like ... uh, like, a couple weeks ago for the stock cars." "Home. Town. *Brother*!" A fourth handshake. I tell him it's so weird to meet somebody from Leavenworth out here that it's breaking my brain in half and he says, "Yeah man, me and my buddy Stevie Durkin drove out here from Lev'worth three years ago for that dry Arizoney climate and we ain never look back. Muh. *Fucker*. I miss it *today*! I can hear the cars right *now*. Vrrroom! Yeah! Woop! Woop! And them *nachos*! Naaaachos! Get your nachos, muhfuckers! Get your nachos right here! You know Stevie, Stevie Durkin? Big guy but got a little baby head and a mouse voice like Michael Jackson? Prison guard out at Lansing? Worked at Petro Deli for a moment. Drunk Stevie? Trouble Stevie?" "I don't know anybody." "You know that auto shop down on 4th that has the, like ... the fuckin' ... what is it called ... that fuckin' ... fuckin' *LED sign* out front with all them Jesus jokes?" "Jesus what?" "*Jesus jokes*, man! Like, God sent the first text message—the bible. That sorta thing. The Easter Bunny never died for nobody's sins. *Jesus jokes*."

"Oh yeah, course! It's like five minutes from the farm where I live." "Stevie's uncle Jarmaine *owns* that place, man! He owns it! Lakeside Speed Waaaayne!" he shouts. I think of shouting my own name, but then I realize I have no reason to. You've got to do something heroic or say something cool in order to shout your own name. People who shout their own name for no reason make everyone else nervous.

26 • "Man, Bozic, what you doin' out in Yuma? You are ... *far* off course, my fren." "I'm on tour all summer." "Like in a band? You play music? *What* instrument?" "No, a book tour. I'm on a book tour." "You got any of your books with you?" I pretend like he's asking if I have my books with me in the river and I make a startled face and act shocked, "What?! Here in the river?! No!" "Hahahaha, I like you, man. *Here in the river.* I like you." "I'm just playin' but yeah, yeah, I got some in my car. I got a bunch of boxes. I'll give you a copy if you want." "*Give.* Shit, man, I'll *trade* somethin' for it. You like long-sleeve t-shirts?" "Sure, yeah, I guess I like long-sleeve shirts." "I got a lotta long-sleeve t-shirts in my van. I'll hook you *up.*"

27 • Digging in the sand for another rock to skip, I find a tiny clam the size of a marble. I pull it dripping from the water— black and yellow with elegant circular ridge lines on its shell like a thing carved from gold. "Check it out. It's a *clam*," I say. I hand it to him. "What the fuck, man, a little bitty clam. What up, little clam? How you doin', muhfucker," he holds it close to his left eye and says, "Man, Bozic, you ever eat a clam?" "Yeah, when I was a kid. Clams and linguine." "Man, it's like eatin' a damn eyeball. I do *not* approve. Clams are cool, though, man. Clams are some chill muhfuckers. You gotta respect a clam.

Just sittin' there and bein' like, *Hey, assholes, I'm a clam and I don't care about shit, leave me alone, get outta here, fuck off because I'm a clam, I ain even got a face.* Man, I wish we was clams. That'd be fuckin' *tight*, man. To be inside *this* little shell? Don't even get me *started*! Let's be *clams.* That's what I'm *talkin'* about, man."

28 • Yeah. Okay. Why not.

29 • Let us be clams.

30 • Two sleepy clams. Let us sleep in the sand and grit and silt. The river flowing above. The breeze rustling the cattails as soft as a dream. The train passing over.

31 • After I trade a book for a shirt with Lakeside Speed Wayne, I sleep for a while on my towel in the sand under the train bridge—a deep, stagnate, dreamless sleep. When I wake up it's dusk and cooler now. Gnats hang in thick clouds over the river water which moves so slow you can hardly tell it's moving. The water is dark like wine bottle glass—glossy, smooth. The sky is shades of gray and purple—aluminum, fireplace ash, orchid, a shadowy violet. The silence, heavy.

32 • That night I eat a couple oranges I pulled off a tree in San Angelo and a bag of Gardetto's rye chips then sleep in the backseat of my car in the parking lot. When I wake up it's

morning and hot again and the sun glares hard through the window.

33 • I take another dip in the river. Then, half-asleep still, I drive back through town wearing my damp swim trunks and the white long-sleeve Dale Earnhardt Jr. shirt Lakeside Speed Wayne traded me.

34 • Driving down the dusty main street—old cars parked in front of vacant storefronts, windows soaped white, signs that read: "We Have Moved," "Sorry We're Closed," "For Rent." A mannequin woman—naked and without hair, armless, leaning in the second story window of a red brick building. On the radio the DJ says, "Whut up, y'all! Iss y'girl Karen Kay! KTTI Yuuuuma! Gon be a *hot* one today. High of 105! Awready *80* and iss only 9:30! Keep cool, drink lotsa water, Yuma. Up next we got Reba. We got *Garth*. We got Kenny Chesney and Alan Jackson and Faith *Hill*. Keep y'dial on KTTI Yuma, Country Hits of Yesterday and Today! Don't go nowhere!"

35 • Don't go nowhere.

36 • I won't.

37 • Driving. My phone sits on the seat next to me—dead black screen, cracked. Battery ran down two days ago. Won't hold a charge.

38 • Driving. The pillowy sand dunes and the sunbaked rock flats. The blazing yellow sun and the great piercing sky, blue and empty of clouds.

39 • Stopped again. Dry wind cooling the sweat in my hair, rattling tin signs nailed to the old gas station facade at Crossing Snake Junction where I pull over for a fill-up and another bag of Gardetto's for later. Getting back in my car my brain says, *Don't go nowhere* in the voice of the KTTI DJ and then I say it out loud in my own voice to no one in particular.

40 • Don't go nowhere. Low hills—blue and dim like strips of faded construction paper. Jagged stone ruins of wasteland settlements.

41 • Don't go nowhere—go somewhere. Hot asphalt and silver pools of heat mirage wriggling on the road up ahead.

42 • Sand dunes as far as you can see. Sand like yellow-white soft serve ice cream, rippling out in all directions, rising in great waves of mounds, dipping into smooth, soft valleys. Driving with my knees, I roll my red bandana into a thin strip and tie it across my forehead to keep the hair and sweat out of my eyes and I think of Bruce Springsteen. Bruce with his red bandana headband, his Fender Telecaster slung low, his cut-off sleeves and some sort of black leather vest, one fist punched in the air, singing about blowing away the lies that leave you lost and brokenhearted, about tearing the pain right

out of your heart because you are done fucking around, you are done hurting yourself, you are fixing what's broke. Out the open window I yell "Bruuuce!" and it feels good to yell it and—

43 • —and out the open window it's tan-yellow desert flats passing. Hills in the distance, absent of feature, boundless south to Mexico. I want to yell "Bruuuce!" a thousand times. I want to claw into my chest and rip out all that's been darkening my eyes.

44 • Rip it all out. That feeling where it's like you're excluded from everything. Where you're disposable to the people you love. Where you're here on the edge fighting like hell to break in, but you can't get through. Where no one *wants* you to get through. Where there's something wrong with you and everyone can *tell* there's something wrong with you and they keep their distance. You don't sleep enough. You always look tired. You say awkward shit that makes you sound stupid. You're bad at keeping in touch. You're weird in a way they don't like. They smell it on you. They see it in your eyes.

45 • Rip it all out. The hard days where you smash your head into a wall from dawn to dusk and stay up all night worried sick with awful gnawing thoughts. Rip it all out. Thoughts like *But you will DIE someday.*

46 • Rip it all out.

47 • Rip it all out. This stupid fucking book tour I'm on and three days ago in Austin where only two people showed up and they were drunk. They sat in the front row and talked to each other about how much they loved movies about whales the whole time until I adlibbed a part in the reading where I said, "I fucking hate whales, I wish they would all get their asses kicked," even though I actually *love* whales, and have always loved whales. The two people got up and one of them said, "Bro you are the worst person in the *world*," and they left and there was no one to read to.

48 • Rip it all out.

49 • Rip it all out. How you never know what to say and sometimes you say something and you're like, "Ugh, no, why did I just *say* that! I am the dumbest person who ever lived. I should be in jail!"

50 • Rip it all out.

51 • Rip it all out. The weight of fear. The weight you've let hold you down like a huge rock chained to your leg, and you're just below the surface of the water fighting for breath, trying to swim up to the air. You can see the light above and the bottom of your boat floating on the surface, but the stone and the chain hold fast.

52 • Rip it all out.

53 • Rip it all out because it feels good. It feels like a sun rising inside you. A lovely yellow flower opening like a gift in your heart.

54 • Driving.

55 • Desert sky as seen through the window—sharp blue against tan and gray. Up ahead of me is a white Mack truck. I pull behind it, but there are cars in either lane and I can't pass.

56 • On the back of the trailer is a crudely drawn black and white image—some sort of magnet poster of an angry man as seen from the chest up, life-size. He looks like a cop and he's pointing a finger in my direction and the caption above his head reads, "HAVE YOU PRAYED TODAY." No question mark. I roll up the sleeves of Lakeside Speed Wayne's Dale Jr. shirt—one, then the other, and when I do that I realize the shirt's a bootleg. Dale is spelled "Dial." I say it out loud and it sounds like an Australian accent. "Dial Earnhardt Jr." I say, "Dial Earnhardt Jr., mate." I say, "Throw a shrimp on the barbie, Dial Jr. Come and say G'day, Dial Jr." It feels good to say and I can't stop saying it and doing so out loud (and *alone*) makes me feel absolutely disconnected from the world and reality and from any chance I've got at being a functioning member of society. Disconnected and thirsty. "Pull ovah for a bee-uh, Dial Jr. *Fosters*, Australian for *bee-uh*. Get a bee-uh for Jiff Gordon, too."

57 • I hit the turn signal and take the off-ramp to get a cold drink. The air is hot and forceful in thick gusts through my window, but now it's easing as I slow and pull up behind a gray van with silver-white glares of sun on its twin back windows, blinding. You can smell the exhaust from its muffler—sour and dark and hot in the air.

58 • I make a left into the parking lot. A group of children are standing in the shade of the entrance to the gas station's Country Kitchen. One of them holds a small dog and the others crowd around to pet it.

59 • I open the car door and step into the heat.

60 • Leaving the mini-mart with my 99-cent bag of popcorn and a can of Country Time lemonade I see a girl with lavender hair stretching in the shade next to the pumps. In the passenger seat of her car, a guy her age is looking at his phone.

61 • The girl dips forward in a bow, then rising graceful, arms skywards in a U shape. She bows at the waist again, swinging her torso to the left before rising back up. Her lavender hair sways left then right.

62 • A man with big eyeglasses and a skinny brown mustache, his thin hair lifting with the breeze like a mohawk, stands next to his Honda Accord, holding the gas nozzle in place as

it pumps into his tank. He's watching her stretch, his necktie flapping over his shoulder in the dry wind, yellow sweat stains under the arms of his shirt. He bends over, reaching into the open window, pulls a tan suede cowboy hat out of the car, and jams it on his head. After that he takes a vape pen out of the pocket of his loose khakis and sucks on it deeply, his cheeks hollowing. I look down before he lets out the smoke.

63 • Sitting in my car in the gas station parking lot I write a postcard to Alison back on the farm and then one to Frankie's boys, my god-sons, who I helped raise until they moved up to Michigan three years ago. I tell Alison about Lakeside Speed Wayne and Dial Jr. and about the Navajo train kids who took me swimming outside Sedona in a great desert canyon, a place called "the Cheese Grater" because you slide down a gushing shoot of wet rocks to the pools below and it shreds your skin and then drops you into an icy pool of water only it's not icy anymore because your heart is racing and the air is hot even at this altitude. You lie floating in the pool and your scraped-up back and sides ache like hell and you stare up at the red canyon walls and *god* you've never felt better. I tell the boys about the abandoned stripmalls and the gas stations selling dried rattlesnake heads and scorpions in glass paperweight baubles. As I write, I eat the popcorn. It tastes like nothing, like styrofoam peanuts that squeak as you bite into them. My throat is dry and it's been dry all day. I crack open my can of lemonade and take a sip, but it doesn't help.

64 • Driving up into the hills of Devil's Canyon before the descent down the pass into Pine Valley, the road twists through the Jacumba Mountains to the summit, boulders strewn on

either side, the land hard and irregular like a great handful of rocks dropped from the sky with no semblance of design. My car struggles with the incline as big rigs pass and disappear up the grade, the road twisting through sharp switchbacks. Below me in the canyon crevice is the rust-blacked carcass of an old van on its side. I look down at it as I drive. My dry throat feels like the metal of that van—coarse, hard. No way anyone survived that fall. It must've rolled a quarter mile, tumbling end over end before it came to rest. Maybe it's fine. Maybe they pushed it over the edge then walked away. Can someone push a van off a cliff? How many people would it take? Ten? They'd have to be weightlifters. Ten weightlifters pushing a van until it tips and rolls tumbling down the cliff. I imagine the weightlifters celebrating after they push the van off the cliff. High-fiving. Flexing. Showing each other their muscles. Maybe one of them is Arnold Schwarzenegger and he's their leader. He says, "Hasta la vista, baby" to the van and his friends high-five some more, flex some more. Maybe one of the weightlifters claps Arnold on the back and tells him, "Don't go nowhere" as a response to "Hasta la vista, baby" and maybe Arnold has a moment of clarity, maybe Arnold thinks, *Don't go nowhere means don't die. Don't go nowhere means don't go to the place that is nowhere. Live, stay alive, pump iron until you're Mr. Universe, make movies, flex your muscles so everyone can see, smoke cigars, take vitamins, crack jokes about killing your enemies in the action movies you star in, drink mineral water, travel back to the past and try to terminate someone, do a sweet family comedy that makes everyone cry and also smile, tell them "Hasta la vista, baby," tell them "I eat Green Berets for breakfast and right now I'm very hungry," tell them "I'll be back" and then BE back, pump more iron, be a governor, be great, be fantastic.* For some reason it makes me want to eat all the spaghetti in the world. I don't know why but it does. I think of a giant plate of cartoon spaghetti with red sauce on top and a couple meatballs and a fork sticking out of it.

65 • Driving.

66 • Driving alone and you get weird thoughts and you realize it's *because* you're alone and you tell yourself you're a complete and total dumb-ass for doing this tour alone and that no one should ever tour on their own. You can't even point out interesting garbage on the side of the road or make up in-jokes or share a hotel room and order pizza and watch TV shows you would never watch in real life. TV shows about angry men who own pawn shops and yell at each other or ugly women who are rich or people who hang out in the jungle naked and fight.

67 • Driving. If I weren't alone I'd turn "Don't go nowhere" into the greatest tour in-joke ever. We'd say, "Don't go nowhere" as we drove through these hard mountains above the desert floor and we'd laugh and we'd use it as "Goodbye!" and as "I love you!" and as a testament to survival. I think of everyone in my life who could be in this car with me. I think about how much better this would be were I not alone—alone driving and not talking for days, alone living off rye chips and Country Time, alone in my rattletrap car with boxes of books I can't sell and an uncharged phone with a shattered screen. I think about the places I could be that aren't this tour, places with people I love. I think about how stupid adults are for doing things like this and I think about how much smarter I was when I was a kid and that makes me think of Frankie's

boys. In my bag in the backseat I have a letter I wrote them before leaving the farm. I've sent the boys postcards this trip but not the letter. Maybe it's not a letter to them at all. Maybe it's a letter to me, written to put in words a line of thinking (and rethinking, *overthinking*) that was hurting me.

68 • Yes, that's how it is.

69 • The goal then was to defuse, release—to pull out the stinger.

70 • The letter reads, "I hope when you're older you remember your early days with me, and I hope what you remember is good. I hope you have a life where they want nothing but happiness for you, where no one will use your name as a joke or as an insult. There's a storm rolling in over Weston. I can see it from the front window of the farmhouse. There's the corner where you stuck stickers of a smiling lion and a giraffe. There's the doorway you walked through and stood in your footie pajamas watching me work when this room was an office; the light pale in the morning and the smell of scrambled eggs your mother cooked you. It's quiet here now and you are away. I hope in Portland your father is treating you well. I hope he goes easy on you. I hope you are laughing somewhere in a clean room with sunlight through the windows, a nice day ahead of you, a sweet morning behind."

71 • I reach the summit of the pass and then I'm headed

down the grade. Out my window it's blue sky and a rising and dropping line of piled rock—the brown and gray stone of the cliff-side, sometimes a wall of it as I take a southward switchback, then sky and the faint details of pinelands in the valley below as I head north.

72 • The air is cooler now, but it's dry—the kind of dry that stings your nostrils, that gives you nosebleeds.

73 • I roll my window down, but it gets stuck halfway. The fuses in my car are dying one by one, blinking out like the tiny lights of a town at night as seen from far away. I try the passenger window. No luck.

74 • Years ago, in the valley below, my parents and a few of their friends took all the kids on a trail ride. An hour in, the guide turned his horse around and rode back to us. He told us not to panic but he'd been watching a mountain lion on the ridge who'd been following us the past twenty minutes. He said, "I figured she'd quit after a while, but she's kept on. Just turn your horses around and we'll all act calm and ride back the way we came. I'm sorry to end it this quick. That lion's *stalkin'* us—she wants the little ones." The lion, he called it a lion, and she, he called it she, wanted the little ones, which meant us kids. Quiet and orderly we rode to the stable and at the lodge the guide gave our money back.

75 • As I descend into the valley I can smell the pine trees and

the dry grasslands and something beyond that, something like water, a lake in the midst of the pines or a pond somewhere I can't see. I imagine a mountain lion standing at the lakeshore, dipping its head down to take a drink.

PART

TWO

THE GREAT SPRING FLOOD

Spring, 2019

1 • I'm in an empty sports bar with Alison and Ethan. It's a quarter past noon in Lincoln, Nebraska, and we're talking about the flooding. Ethan's wife So-hyun stands at the counter at the other end of the bar ordering a drink—her form losing shape with the sunlight streaming in from the big front windows. She laughs, rocking her head back, but the music is loud and you can't hear what she's laughing about. Alison says, "All the way up here you'd see what you thought was the river, but then there'd be rooftops and it's like, *Wait, that was a town*." The bar smells like stale beer, vinegar, and french fries. It's not a bad smell.

2 • An older woman, stick-thin and tanned dark brown in acid wash blue jeans, flip flops, and a sleeveless pink shirt walks past our table on the way to the restrooms talking on her phone, saying, "I doan wanna watch *none* of that Star Wars spaceman Dark Vader robot-ass shit. I'm goin' to *Risky's*."

3 • Ethan takes a sip of his beer, sets it back on the tabletop in front of him, and says, "There are corn and soybean fields west and north of here that won't be farmable for *generations*. Top soil's washed away." Ethan wears a checked blue and white cowboy shirt and his dark blonde hair is shorter than I'd seen him last. His beard is close-cut, not trimmed but tidy. He looks healthy, relaxed, younger than I remember him, like he's aging in reverse, but also more squared-away—composed, grounded. Ethan's been working as a cannabis industry journalist out in Denver the past couple years. He has a great job, a good truck, and a nice place just outside the city. It seems as if life is working out for him in ways that it's not working out for me and Alison. So-hyun walks back from

the bar, slim and pretty in jeans and a black tank top with her cocktail, which glows hot orange from the late-in-the-day sunlight behind her. "You makin' friends?" asks Ethan, smiling at her, attentive, loving. "Oh, *always*," she says. Ethan and So-hyun met when he was working a newspaper job in Seoul. They're very natural together; comfortable around each other. So-hyun the hip, sophisticated city girl from a good Korean family and Ethan the Nebraska farm-kid-turned-successful-journalist. They're a perfect match. Different but well-paired.

4 • The streets of Lincoln are hot and crowded as dusk settles in—college kids coming in and out of the bars and ice cream parlors and pizza shops. Families having a Sunday on the town. A band loading into a club up a ways. Four sweaty, tired-looking guys our age in black jeans and t-shirts carrying amps and drum cases. A tall, thin, clean-cut man in a fashionable gray suit walks toward us pushing a double stroller with two sleeping toddlers. He's wearing huge brown-lensed sunglasses that look like they're from the '70s or something a grandma once owned and he's talking on his phone. As he passes he tells the person on the other end of the line, "Vicki's got a serious problem with shellfish." In the sky to the west is an arcade of heavy, dark clouds—leaden sky, purple like a bruise, thunderheads nearly black, thick with rain.

5 • I smell the rain in the air and the wet blacktop and my mind goes to an image of three small arrowheads on my grandfather's dresser. Mud-red stone, smooth like river rocks. He found them on the grassy ridge above his farm in La Veta, Colorado—a beautiful, quiet place with the Spanish Peaks dim in the haze. This happens often when I smell rain. A flash of

color and memory and a feeling of both mystery and security. It leads to other things—an image of my grandfather's .22 pistol, an old blue steel cowboy revolver in his sock drawer. The taste of cherry Kool-Aid and the dark ruby light shining through the round pitcher in the sun. The smell of horses. The smell of coffee brewing before I'd tasted coffee and eggs fried in bacon fat in my grandparents' kitchen. The sound of the wind through the prairie grass on the ridge, a sound closer to silence than noise, and a brown horse off in the distance walking along the fence-line. On a telephone pole up ahead of us is a cardstock poster with a photo of Ethan. It says his name and then "Reading from his new book and works yet unpublished on April 6th, 2019. Come join us!" Under that in a smaller font it says, "Acclaimed emerging author" and "A new voice of the modern Western experience." In the photo he stares intently at the camera. There's humor in his eyes. It's a good picture. We pass the poster without saying anything about it and walk into the air-conditioned bookstore, Ethan opening the door for us.

6 • After Ethan's reading—a table of half-finished plates of food, beer bottles, and cocktails in a loud Thai restaurant with some of his college friends. Alison in braids and a blue and white striped, button-up cowgirl shirt knotted in front telling a story about a place we drove past on the way here called the Museum of Shadows. She says, "The sign was like, 'Voted the most haunted museum in the world' and I thought, *What, who's on the voting panel for something like that because sign me up.*" She holds the red dimpled-glass candle in her hands as she talks, sliding it back and forth across the white tablecloth, the light flickering as the candle moves. I sit and watch her talk and everything falls away. I watch her mouth, the light and humor in her dark blue eyes as she smiles. I'm

drunk and I hate that I'm drunk, but I let it go away and I think the kinds of loose, generous thoughts you do when you've had too much. Ethan and So-hyun sit across from us and they're laughing at what Alison says and I'm proud that they're laughing. Ethan's friends at the end of the table lean closer. They're smiling, faces flushed with drink. I wave at our server and point down at my empty glass and make the sign for one more.

7 • Alison says, "So, on the way up here we had a detour. I mean, yeah, there were a million detours because the 29 was closed just after St Joe, but we left the interstate and crossed this great big enormous steel bridge over the river and I looked back and *holy fuckin' shit,* dude, it was a riverboat half sunk and the water all raging up around it and surging over the sides." "Dude, no way, like a real riverboat?" asks one of Ethan's friends. "Yeah, for sure, a no-shit old-timey Mark Twain Tom Sawyer Faulkner steamship riverboat. Y'know, with a big ol' fuckin' paddle wheel in the back and three-stories of decks and double smoke stacks and it's leaning halfway over with one side up in the air and the river was going like a hundred miles an hour with the flood and then we made a right turn and our view of it was gone. We went up into the hills and probably only … we saw it for what … what, maybe five seconds?" I shrug and she continues, "But it was just this … this … this stark, like, *desperate* scene out of an old Southern gothic novel. My heart was racin' like crazy. When we got up into the hills you could look down at the valley and it was water—water as far as you can see, brown muddy water, and the tops of trailers, rooftops, telephone poles, just a whole *sea* in the valley where the town once was."

8 • I sit back and I shut my eyes and rub the bridge of my nose

between my thumb and forefinger and a sea of noise floats up to surround me, rising around our table like dark water until I hear nothing but the murmur and hush of voices and the sound of forks and knives scraping plates and bussers clanking stacks of dishes they carry off to the kitchen and the music far off behind that. Just then a woman's voice behind me breaks through the sound, a rasping smoker's voice. "He was my *boss* when we met. Until we got married." Then her tablemate, in a voice nearly identical, "Now *you're* the boss!" and wild cackling laughter from them both. I open my eyes and Alison is looking at the bill, leaning over the tabletop to write in the tip.

9 • It's raining like hell when we say goodbye outside the last bar of the night. Ethan's group walks one way and Alison and I the other. We stick under the storefront awnings, running in the streetlight-lit spaces between them. It stops raining once we're on the road, but it's a dark night—foggy too, cars emerging out of the wall of gray just as they pass you, late-night stragglers like ourselves, solitary big rigs, cops looking for drunks. Out in the country there's no one and I drive fast while Alison sleeps—dark fields and farmhouses passing by buried back behind the fog. A stretch of deep woods where you see nothing but the beams of your own headlights on the black patch of asphalt in front of you, mist speckling the window, and the wiper blades clunking side to side, fog in clouds we burst through. I sing along with the car stereo, quietly, but it feels good. There's a certain pleasure in singing your favorite songs on a long drive when you're not alone, but no one is awake to listen to your tuneless voice. I sing about going out to Denver to see what I can't find and I sing about when you're lost in the rain in Juarez and it's Easter time, too. I sing about the room of my house where the light's never been and I sing

that I thought of you as my mountaintop, thought of you as my peak.

10 • I sing along with country songs my grandparents played in Colorado when I was a child. The stories of John Hardy when he was a baby and that hypocritical Harper Valley PTA and how sonofagun we're gonna have big fun on the bayou. That Colorado farmhouse where I sat under the dining room table with my toy cars, and my grandfather Cecil came in from his woodshed smelling like pine sawdust. I heard his cowboy boots on the floorboards and then a man on the record player with a hard, nasally voice singing, "how's about cookin' somethin' up for me-eee," and my grandpa singing along and from the kitchen my grandmother Drusilla and my great-grandmother Bess laughing. They were making corn fritters—dough fried with pieces of sweet corn, little yellow cookie-size cakes, to which there is no equal.

11 • The track ends and there's silence and I can hear the rain speckling the window and the thump of the wipers switching back and forth. The next song is from one of my former tour-mates, Joelly Bell. It's the first single off his latest (and final) record—the record that was released the week the statements from his victims hit the internet. I'd cleared his tracks off my phone, but this one must have missed the cut. It's a song I used to like—a song about being a fair and just person, about looking for a world where people are softer to each other. A world that seemed possible until we found out the things he'd done. Two-faced Joelly. Like a televangelist fleecing his flock, tears streaming down his face in rivers at the pulpit, arms raised to the Lord. What was *Joelly's* Lord? Power. It

was power over people once he'd gained their trust. I reach down to the phone wedged between the seat and my left thigh and skip the track forward. The next song is another country song. It's about silver wings shining in the sunlight. I turn it up and sing along, changing the lyrics to "Lakeside Speed Waaayne shining in the sunlight/Lakeside Speed Wayne/ headed somewhere in flight." What a wide space seems to lie between tonight and that day floating in the river just a year past. A lost, wayward summer—sand dunes, glaring sun, the heat rippling the air, lonesome mornings in desert towns. Now—darkness, windshield wipers, rain, woods.

12 • At the truck stop in the junction the aisles are bright-lit and it feels a world away from the dark road outside and the dark cab of my car with Alison sleeping peacefully under my denim jacket and my favorite songs playing. I pass a rack of gaudy pre-weathered cowboy hats and a display case full of novelty knives in the shape of pistols and a series of lighters shaped like shotgun shells. I grab a bag of rye chips for me and Bugles for Alison next to a spinner rack of bumper stickers and then turn the rack, reading the slogans. "Sorry if my patriotism offends you. Trust me, your lack of spine offends me" with an image of a body-armored soldier holding a machine gun, his face hidden behind goggles and a cloth mask, a tattered American flag behind him. "My dog is a democrat. He waits around all day and expects me to feed him." "If you don't stand behind our troops, feel free to stand in front of them." "Keep honking, I'm reloading." "I'd rather be a conservative nut job than a liberal with no nuts or job." "I support LGBTQ. Liberty, guns, bible, Trump, BBQ" in bold white text over the image of a Confederate flag. "Warning, driver is armed." Someone is making popcorn in the back. I hear it popping and then it's the chime of the microwave and the air smells buttery

with a bit of stale, sour burn.

13 • I stand at the checkout awhile before a teenage girl comes out from the back room with a big blue plastic bowl of popcorn. She's wearing a camo ball-cap pulled low over her eyes and an oversized red t-shirt with the words "Keep Calm and Carry Firearms" in white lettering. She sets the bowl underneath the counter. "Sorry t'keep you waitin' 'n' all. I'm stressin' out and I need somethin' t'munch on." "Yeah?" "My grandaddy's farm's under four feet'a water and they let their flood insurance lapse last year." "Damn. Sorry." "I cain't believe this shit. This rain ever gon stop?" "I hope so." "Yeah, me too. Uh, sorry, four fifty. Cash?" "Credit." "Y'all ain gettin' gas?" "No, I'm good." "The chip reader doan work. You just slide it." "Okay. Cool." A tall, older, heavyset man in a dripping wet straw hat and rain-spotted overalls comes through the front entrance and the bell over the door dings. "Hey Cassie! Hoo! That *rain*!" When he talks I notice he has no teeth. He says, "Iss comin' down! Hoo! Howsyer folks?" "*Oh* you know. Cain't catch a break. This weather 'n' all." "Ohhhh you *know* I know, sweetie. You know I know. It's been inneresting *times*. You and yours are in my prayers, babygirl." "I 'ppreciate that, Mr. Combs. Give my love t'Katie Lou, okay?" "I shall, I shall. She'll be pleased to know you been thinkin' of her. Hey, where you got your SpaghettiOs?" "Second aisle next t'the dog food and beans."

14 • It's raining harder now. I run outside with the back of my t-shirt pulled up over my head, yank the door open, and dump myself into the car seat. Alison is awake, looking at her phone, the pale glow on her face. "Whew, crazy, look how wet I got runnin' ten feet." "It safe to drive?" "I think so. You get good sleep?" "I wasn't sleeping that much. At first I was,

but then I was just kinda lyin' there with my eyes closed."
"I thought you were asleep. I was singing my head off like
a moron." "No, it was nice. What'd you get?" "Gardetto's,
Bugles for you, and a yellow drink." I nod down at the tall
can between my thighs then snap the tab open with the nail
of my forefinger. "You're on a yellow drink kick." "I guess I
am." "Well, Mr. Yellow Drink, get us on home." She snuggles
back into the sleeping position and pulls my denim jacket
over her. "Okay, on home we go." I put the car in reverse and
we back out of the parking spot.

15 • Home on the farm. Quiet days while the rain keeps coming.
The fields in the lowlands flood until taking the highway to the
city is like driving on a land-bridge over a dead ocean. The
summer corn crop is ruined. Fields are left unplanted. The
Missouri River keeps rising. It crests the banks at the Fort
and floods the campground. The schools close. Roads close.
Ranchers move their cattle and horses to higher ground. A
Kansas City Star newspaper article reads, "Serenity Ranch
owner Clint Nimmo said the flood was like a scene out of a
horror movie." "Nimmo said spiders and centipedes were
crawling up the walls and onto their backs to escape the
water." Headlines read, "Who is to blame for the floods?" and
"Cost of river flooding already tops $1 billion." On Saturday I
get a check for books sold to balance out my negative account.
I leave the farm and drive to the grocery store in town with
my wipers beating side to side, but I can't see much beyond
the front of my car. Standing in the freezer section looking
at the tater tots I hear an older man say into his phone, "This
whole damn *world's* gone to hell and I know *why*." I listen for
the why, but he starts talking about microwaveable chicken
instead. "What you gotta know 'bout microwaveable chicken
is it's all in the *technique*. Microwaveable chicken ain't any

worse than normal chicken if you're smart about it. There's a trick to the settings. You cook it on Popcorn setting for the first minute then Roast for the next minute then Potato for the rest. It's a game you gotta play." I buy sourdough bread, avocados, tater tots, red grapes, limes, spinach, corn tortillas, pinto beans, mushrooms, vegetable bouillon, black olives, Ragu marinara sauce, Barilla angel hair pasta, and a jar of my favorite MaraNatha almond butter I can never afford.

16 • Water—you think of it carving canyons and you think of it raising coffins from the ground and floating them like boats in the surge.

17 • Another trailerpark washed away. "Where I come from rain is a good thing" goes a country song on the radio because rain makes corn and corn makes whiskey and whiskey makes his baby feel a little bit frisky. Meanwhile the world grows outside in tangles and thickets, the prairie grass shoulder-high, the trees heavy with new leaves and ivy vining up over the walls of the farmhouse and honeysuckle in masses along the road. You smell it when the wind is right, sweet and verging on rot.

18 • Once, years ago, taking the train across country for Frankie's dad's military retirement, we saw a flashflood in the New Mexico desert. For a while the stream of water raced alongside the train in an old dry creek-bed. We'd outrun it and then it would catch up to us again. We watched the tail-end of the water chasing out across the dry ground like the long tongue of some old beast, forked and

then solid, lapping up the banks as it grew in force, dark brown against the pale yellow sand and the gray rock banks of the creek bed. In the sky to the north of the track was a mass of black clouds, electricity coursing through it in hot-white crags and jagged bright veins as it moved toward us. We were in a sleeper car. The attendant had just cleared our breakfast plates and we sat in seats opposite each other with our books. Frankie had a copy of Swanberg's *Citizen Hearst* and mine was *A Moveable Feast*, but we didn't read. We watched the flood, and then we outran it once more and after that we didn't see it again.

19 • Alison and I sit up late at the kitchen table eating tater tot and guacamole tacos while the rain comes down and I tell her the story my great-aunt Dilly told me about her grandfather in the Johnstown Flood of 1889. How all the neighbors lost their homes but theirs was okay so it became the local morgue. They laid the bodies of their neighbors on every bed until they had to use the floor and you couldn't walk through the rooms without stepping on someone you knew. There were stories of naked bodies twisted up in wreckage or stuck hanging by the leg from trees. Whole houses carried downstream then left intact. Rail lines washed away. Lives washed out of existence. "There's this story Dilly told about her grandfather clearing some land for grazing a month after the flood and finding a man buried up to his shoulders in a great expanse of dried, cracked mud, still wearing his straw hat, head bowed a little like he was taking a snooze, only he was dead. He got up closer and the man's face was badly decomposed, but he realized it was Ovid Barkus, one of the coal miners he'd worked with for years. Dilly said her uncle Efrem told a story about a man coming to his door one night around the time of the First World War asking for water and when he gave him a glass

he drank it then walked off into the night without saying anything else. Efrem said it was Ovid Barkus, that same man Dilly's grandpa came across in the field of mud. He said his eyes looked like black wet holes in his head."

20 • In the morning the thunderstorms darken the house like it's still night. Outside it's greenish silver sky and the boughs of the oak and black walnut trees thrashing in the wind. I sit at the old redwood table in the front room and light a candle and it's dark dark dark and I think maybe it would be great if it were dark like this always. But of course that would be awful. Dark like this is good and you can take that and be happy with it and feel a rush of thrill when it's happening. It's like the day of the eclipse when Alison and I and her sweet back-home friend Eugene Cone drove out into the cornfields and sat on top his rental van and watched the darkness sweep over the plains until you couldn't see your hand in front of your face. There was an SUV in the field parked next to us with three teenage girls and a little boy sitting on top of it just like us and as the darkness fell we couldn't see them anymore, but we could hear them shouting about how dark it was. That was a thrill too, but it came to an end and this is what separates adventure from a meaner reality. Adventures need to end so you can enjoy the ease after the excitement ebbs back. Divisions, opposites, and polarities are important. You can't have home without away. You can't have lovely joy without her cruel sister sadness. A thrill must end so another can begin.

21 • The best storms here come at night. The wildest ones where it feels as if the whole house could rise up and float

away. Float away like Noah and his animals. At night when it storms, the dogs go into a wild, senseless panic like they're losing their minds and I put them in the bathroom and turn on all the lights and the clunky old wall fan. After that it's hard to go back to sleep, so I lie in bed and I will the house to float away.

22 • Float us away.

23 • Float us away to someplace better. Somewhere without prisons up the road and white supremacists in the holler and long, daunting winters and that hard prairie wind that kicks up in the morning and doesn't quit all day. I think of the place my grandparents had after they left Colorado to escape the altitude. That fifth-wheel in the trailerpark between the desert hills and Lake Havasu. The dry air and the rock-strewn landscape and everything as safe and sweet as you could want. Their neighbor Tom Bluefeather, the former college basketball star, 6 foot 8, with his lovely family and the banana cream pies his wife Melinda would bring over. "I made you a banana cream. New recipe. This is the best yet." I think often of the gravel walk to the swimming pool with Tom Bluefeather's daughter Henny Lee who was blind but walked as sure as me. The desert sky so big and baby blue and vast above us. Everyone in the trailerpark saying, "Hiya, kiddos," and "Hello, my little friends," and "Howya doin' Miss Henny Lee and Cecil's lil' grandson? You stop on by JennaLynn's trailer. She made her famous oatmeal raisin cookies again." With neighbors like that why lock your doors? Why sleep poorly at night? The windows wide open. The screendoor clap-clappin' in the breeze. All is good and kind and easy. The

low hills behind the trailerpark, the light blue puddle of the lake in the distance, the sunset a rose gold fantasy. Float us away.

24 • Float us away like Noah and stick us on the side of a mountain with green, sloping pastures and a scouting dove and a big swooping rainbow. Float us away.

25 • Float us away. This is my invocation. A wish and a want. Float us away ...

26 • In a break between rains we go to the spot down by the Missouri River where we usually hunt for fossils, but the water is up to the tree trunks. It's a calm day, not a cloud in the sky, and all you hear is the gurgle of the river eddies where a rockpile or a fallen tree swept downstream makes the current flow circular in a whirlpool. We stand in the woods and watch the brown muddy river move southward. On the opposite bank stands a line of dark trees with the water halfway up their trunks. The water looks alive, it *feels* alive, it feels thick even from our dry spot in the woods, as if swimming in it would be like swimming in pure mud or honey or glue. We walk through the woods and find a paved utility road and head up into the hills. At a lookout point you can see the train-tracks and the trains are still running. We watch a freight-train down below us running along northbound and the river-water lapping just feet from its tracks.

27 • The utility road runs downhill and into the flatlands. On either side of the road, great ponds that were once corn and soy fields stretch out until they reach higher elevation. Up ahead the water from one pond is trickling over the road into the other. Something silvery moves in a wriggling mass across the road.

28 • It's very still in the clearing—quiet except for the sound of the birds shrieking in the mulberry trees. It feels as if the world has ended.

29 • "What *is* that?" Alison says, pointing up ahead. "It looks like *fish*."

30 • We get closer and it's fish alright—thousands of tiny fish swimming in the quarter inch of water against the current from the smaller pond to the larger one. "Look at that," she says, "it's fish crossing the road." They break the surface of the pond and struggle up over the asphalt and race along the road in zigzags as their tiny, beating fins barely grab enough water to make it across. Some clear the road and make it to the bigger pond. Some make it before being swept back. The wet asphalt is covered in little sliver-size dead fish that weren't able to cross and others still gasping for breath. We squat down and help as many as we can over to the bigger pond, but they keep coming. Soon the sun is setting over the trees to the west and there's nothing we can do. "There's just too *many*," Alison says, standing back up, dusting her knees. In the ten-foot patch of wet blacktop thousands of fish fight to cross. The lower pond is full of silvery flashes and green bodies darting in

43

schools. We turn and walk back the way we came.

31 • Driving through the country it's water everywhere you look. Hay fields that are now muddy blue ponds reflecting the sky. Patches of woods gone dark murky swamp. Sometimes on the old Wolcott highway the water floods a dip in the road and blocks your access to the interstate and you turn around and drive back the way you came. Sometimes it's shallow and you drive right through as it begins to rise. When you catch a glimpse of the river as you crest a hill it's higher than you've ever seen it. The day of the eclipse, later that night, Alison and I and Eugene Cone tried to drive through what we thought was a shallow flooded train overpass on the way into Lawrence after a show at the White Schoolhouse. We drove under the overpass and then the water was up to our doors and the engine shut off and the water rose so fast it came pouring in the open windows before we could get our seatbelts off. We climbed out the windows and waded through the water out from under the overpass and stood in the pouring rain and Eugene Cone called for a tow.

32 • In the morning I do farm chores in the rain. First the dogs go out. Bella, the black and white brindle pitbull, and Pumpkin, the akita. Feed them. Bring them back in. Give them fresh water. They're wet and the mudroom has that awful wet dog smell, a bad smell like leather soaked in cat piss and sour milk, but it's a comforting smell. A stinking wet dog is still a good animal, an animal that needs a little time to doze in the warm farmhouse and dry off. By the time I'm pulling my raincoat back on a few minutes later, the dogs are asleep, curled up together on one of the gray dog beds next

to the kitchen's heater vent. My raincoat isn't a raincoat at all. It's an old wool-lined, light blue denim rancher's coat my grandmother Drusilla gave me when my grandfather Cecil passed. It's too big for me, but it's warm and heavy and thick enough to keep you dry. A denim coat as a raincoat is a metaphor on farm life. Unless you've got a great job in the city to fund your lovely, picturesque hobby farm, you probably don't have enough of anything. You make do. You improvise. You build a gate to the chicken yard out of a piece of goat fence. You fix whatever's broke with baling twine, scrap wire, and bent nails you've pulled out of old boards in the barn. You throw on your grandpa's denim coat and you turn up the collar and smash an old straw hat over your head and you go back outside.

33 • Barn cats are next. Feed them in a dry spot where the roof juts out over the back deck. A mason jar of Meow Mix. Two piles. One for the big orange cat Lil' Petey and one for the tiny black one we call Baphomet. Without the wind to push it, the rain comes straight down and it makes puddles in the chicken yard—brown muddy puddles with water drumming into them and splashing back upwards. Water streams off the eaves and pours in thick, dirty spouts from the rain gutters. The rain drips from the brim of my straw hat; the drops quivering on the frayed edge like little gems. It soaks into my work gloves as I unlatch the door of the chickens' lean-to. On dry days they can't wait to fall over each other racing out the door to peck the kitchen scraps I bring. Today they stay put. I toss a mason jar of feed corn onto the yellow matted straw they sleep on and a couple of them hop down from their roosts to peck at it. That's as far as they'll go. Our chickens are like old people who feel the weather in their bones. They're sleepy, desirous of soft pleasures and easy domestic comfort. Until the storm lets up they'll stay inside, warm and safe. If they were people they would be like, "Let's just watch movies and

eat cookies and pizza today, alright?" Next up are the sheep and goats. I close the chicken gate, latch it shut with one of Jude's old climbing carabiners, and open the big red-painted steel gate to the fields. Our barn is a double garage. I pull open the second garage door and the sheep and the goats walk out into the rain—Edie with her long, white, floppy goat ears and her friendly bleat that sounds as if she's saying her name; the fat black and brown Nubian billy goat Andrew with his barrel body; then the sheep, little Beau and the big bruiser Kid, bottlefed wether Gulf Coasts Frankie rescued from slaughter when they were lambs. The four of them troop out into the rainy fields on their thin, knobby, spindly legs without a care in the world. Goats and sheep are hardy creatures. Rain, sun, or snow, they follow their ancient routine—wake, eat, drink water, chew cud, repeat until dusk, then sleep. I watch them as they disappear behind our fence made of red-painted pallets for the better grass in the far field. It's good to be around them. Your heart tells you: *This is something people and animals have been doing for a very long time.*

34 • I go back inside and hang my grandpa's coat on a nail in the mudroom and set my hat on top the washer next to the dusty orange and white box of dryer sheets then shuck off my wet boots. The farmhouse is warm and dry. It's a good house. Rundown but spacious and well cared-for, well-loved. Crystal prisms are hung in the windows to catch the light and refract rainbows on the walls in drifting patches. Dried herbs and flowers bound with twine hang from nails. Books and magazines sit in colorful, disorderly stacks wherever you look. The house smells like jasmine incense and candle wax and old paper. There are brass animals on tables—an eagle with uplifted wings and a proud unicorn sitting amongst glass bowls and pewter trays of minor treasures—roughened cobalt

beach glass, pink agates, yellow and black tiger's eye, polished malachite, carnelian, silvery abalone pearls, blobs of melted copper, fossilized crinoids, Roman coins, Civil War shoe buckles, red glass beads. We've hung mirrors on the walls, small ones shaped like diamonds or Egyptian eyes, strange oval and triangular mirrors with wide brass frames, paintings of bats and horses, faded Proustian still life flowers, preschool art by Frankie's boys that look like impressionist dreams. In every corner and spot of empty window space sits a house plant. Dazzling red poinsettias, thin Norfolk pines that reach to the ceiling, fiddle leaf plants, a bony citronella with its lemon balm smell, healthy African violets; the kitchen windows have black plastic tubs of cooking herbs—cilantro, mint, basil. There are red and green glass vases of purple flowers from the field, sprigs of cut lavender, roses with a winey red splash over pale white. I grab my manuscript off the wooden table in the front room and sit down on the couch. A few minutes later Alison is out of the shower and the house now smells like coconut shampoo, steam, and rose oil. I hear her make coffee, sing quietly to herself. "Santa Baby," a Christmas song out of season. "James, you want tea?" she asks. I tell her I'm okay. "You hungry? You want a banana? I'm having a banana. You should eat a banana." "No, no thanks, I'm alright." Alison comes into the front room dressed for work with a banana in one hand and a travel mug of coffee in the other. "I have to go to work early," she says, then holds the banana in front of her mouth like a frown. I laugh and set my manuscript on the round glass end-table next to me. "Got time to sit?" "I wish." "What time you gettin' out?" "Pretty early. I have a meeting with Darlene at two and then I can leave whenever." "Okay, let's do pasta for dinner. We have angel hair." "Sounds good. Do you want wine? I can get a box on the way home." "Yeah, can you get butter? I think we're out." "We're out. Yeah, yeah, I will. Ugh, I don't want to have to go to *work*. Can't I just go in there and tell 'em I quit?" "I'm sorry. Maybe we'll do a fire tonight—if it stops raining." "That would be nice. If I can't quit let's do that at least." I spend the next five hours working on a scene set in Mexico. A Valentine's Day weekend trip years ago. I think of old friends. Chente Ramirez with his greaser haircut, his switchblade, and his love for Mariah Carey. My ex Julia and her cousin Lacey. Babyfaced kids pretending to be adults. Babies. We were kids. I try to remember the words we said, the food we ate, the joke we would say about a monkey fucking a football, the way things went to hell, the ways we tried to fix them. I try not to worry about money while I do this. I try not to think of unpaid bills and late rent and uncertain futures and the hustle that takes up all the time I don't spend writing. To tell the story I need to tell I'll have to remove myself from where I am and exist solely in memory. I'll need to forget the rain, the couch I'm sitting on, the body I'm in, the walls around me, the ceiling and the tar-shingled roof the rain streams off.

35 • At dusk I do farm chores. The dogs back out. Chickens back in. Goats and sheep up for the night in their cozy barn with its scent of straw and clean pine shavings. The evening work is faster than the morning chores and the rain has stopped which makes it easier. When the work is done I stand at the wire fence with my arms draped over it and stare out into the fields. The pallet fence that divides the upper field in two was painted red by Alison, Frankie, and her boys during the brief time we all lived together. It was after Frankie left Jude but before Frankie and Michael were together. Alison had moved out to Kansas to be with me a couple months earlier. Everything was new or changing and nothing felt bad or heavy or hard. The boys were very young then and they brought their big plastic cars, the type kids ride by straddling

the seat and pushing along with their legs. I remember a calm, warm spring day with the grass as green as bright jade, the sky vast and pale blue and streaked with soft white clouds and the swooping lines of jet contrails. I worked in the garden staking up new tomato plants while Alison and Frankie hammered in t-posts, then slid the pallets up over the posts, and used scrap wire to bind each pallet to its neighbor. After that the four of them painted the pallets a perfect, cheery barn-red—the boys shirtless in their little blue denim toddler overalls, and then the work was done and it was a fine thing to see.

36 • Now the pallets have weathered. The paint has faded. A few of the pallets have busted slats, but all remain upright, sturdy. The fence is still a fence, still a good, strong thing built by human hands. It's a symbol of our past, a past that didn't work out the way we hoped. A past that saw the separation of our group, a painful summer and autumn that sent us our separate ways.

37 • The sun sinks low in the west and now the fields are dark—a line of yellow and pale pink on the horizon over the woods and hills. Behind me the house is lit merrily with squares of gold window light. I see the dark shape of Alison standing in the kitchen window before she moves out of view. Soon it will be time to make dinner. I'll boil and salt the water for the pasta and make a sauce with the tomatoes we put up last summer. I'll use basil and oregano from the garden and a few fresh tomatoes tossed in near the end to contrast the cooked ones. We'll have red wine from a box and buttered sourdough and maybe we'll listen to quiet records while we eat. Country music or maybe Jack Rose, Fahey, Sandy Bull.

After a few glasses of wine my tastes will change and I'll put on the louder stuff from before I was born—the Velvets, the Dolls, Patti, Johnny Thunders, Richard Hell, which will make me think of my friend Chente Ramirez again and that will lead to '50s rock 'n' roll and old doo-wop. (If I'm not careful I'll drink more and then I'll talk about how much I love rock 'n' roll until I cry. There's a line I can't cross and I try very hard to keep from crossing it.) We'll sit at the kitchen table and talk and the edges of the night will fold softly and dim and soon we will sleep.

38 • I walk back to the house and the past is still with me—the pallet fence but also the story I wrote earlier. I know if I'm going to be worth a damn as a functioning human I'll need to shake this off, come back to the present, get myself out of my head, restart the day in order to begin the night. Sometimes it feels like time will loop if you let it—if you think about the past and then the future and then the past again while going about your day in the present. It will come in rolling circles, cycles, repeat, call back, restart, endings to beginnings to endings again.

39 • No, that's bullshit.

40 • That's some been-alone-too-long-today bullshit thinking.

41 • As I walk across the wet grass I hear thunder rolling in the distance—a low, thudding, murmuring grumble.

42 • Frankie comes down to visit from Michigan while her boys are out in Portland with their dad. She and her mom and Alison and I go to the outlet mall and see a movie about people escaping a hurricane who are then attacked by giant alligators. We sit in our big reclining seats and pass a giant bucket of popcorn and a box of Junior Mints and laugh and jump when the alligators lunge out of the water or tear someone's arm off and we talk to the characters on screen. We tell them, "No, don't go in that room, don't you know *anything*?" and we tell them, "Turn around turn around turn around, I can't *believe* this," "Put down that phone you dumb fucking idiot." Of course they don't listen and of course things go from very bad to way worse. This is the first time in two years Frankie and Alison have been in the same room since their falling-out. It was tentative at first, but it's fine.

43 • When the film is over, we walk out of the theater, happy and laughing together. "That was exactly the movie I wanted to see. Alligators are the fucking *best*." "You know just what you're getting when you walk into a movie like that and no matter how bad it is it's fucking *great*." "I started to root for the *alligators* the girl was being so dumb about everything." "They should do another version where it's from the alligators' perspective and the alligators are actually the heroes." "I thought they *were* the heroes."

44 • Outside the theater it's getting late, but the sun hasn't set, and the mall is full of people standing around the fountain and coming in and out of stores with shopping bags. A tall redheaded teenager wearing a green and white basketball uniform leans down over the fountain and drinks from it,

cupping water to his mouth. "*What? Gross. Did that just happen?* What the fuck's wrong with that guy?" says Frankie. Alison and Frankie's mom and I laugh. "That actually happened, like *happened* happened," Alison says, and Frankie's mom says, "Maybe he thinks there's a giant Britta filter under there," and we all laugh again, and then we walk to our cars. By the time we cross the parking lot, the sun is sinking below the rooftops of the hotel and the row of new condos.

45 • The sun is setting and the sky is like orange and vanilla sherbet.

PART
THREE

THE NEW

OLD

WEST

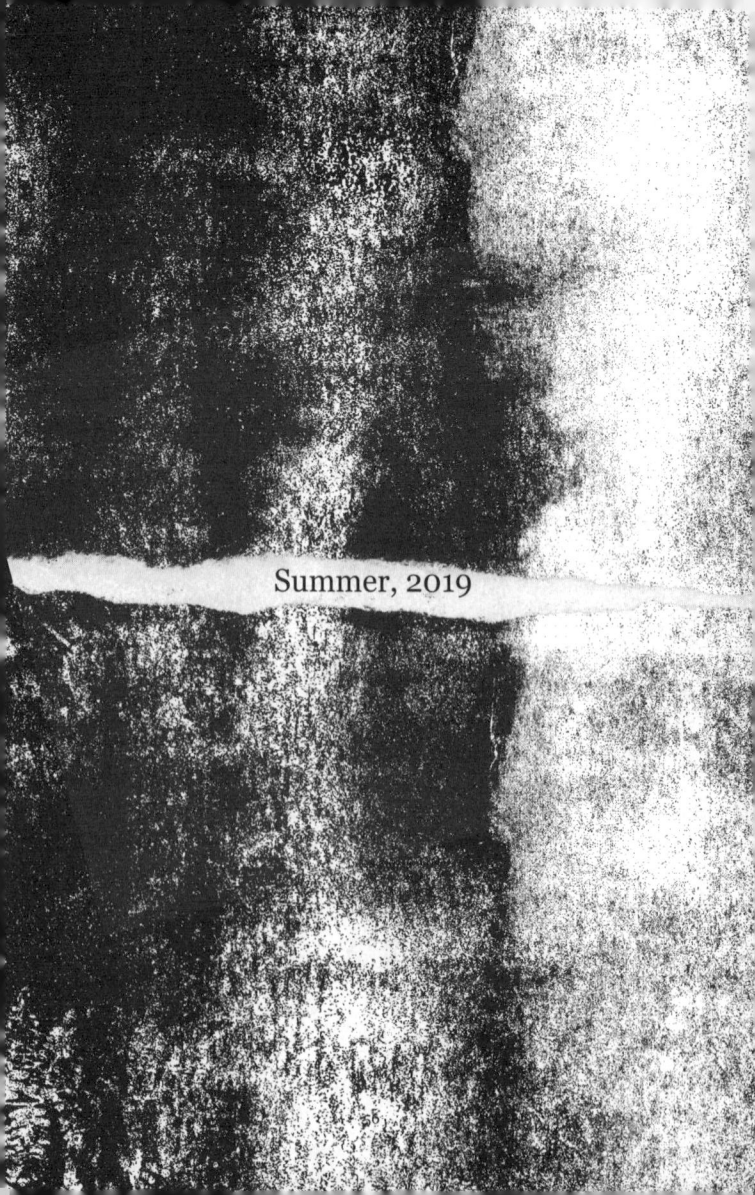

Summer, 2019

1 • Frankie's boys were born at the farm in 2010 and 2012 and they lived here until 2015. There were wheelbarrow rides. Cherry tomato feasts in the garden. We sat in the middle room on days when it was too hot to move and watched their favorite movies on repeat. For weeks we watched a DVD boxset from the Leavenworth library with footage of fire-engines being washed and wrecking ball cranes smashing buildings and garbage trucks with men stepping off the side to heave black plastic trash bags into the backend. I made them peanut butter and jelly sandwich after peanut butter and jelly sandwich. "Saaaanveech!" they would shout, delirious with the joy of loving sandwiches. (Later, their stepfather Michael would nickname them "the Sandwich Brothers.") I carried them when they stuck their arms up at me and said, "Hoad me! Hoad meeee!" I taught them the names of Star Wars characters and listened as they made up songs about coral reefs and cowboys running away from armies of pirates. They would sing things like, "And then the pirates came/And they had a pirate ship and gunses/And the cowboys runned awaaaay/And the pirates chaseded them," and they would sing, "Aaaand the coral reef passed me by when I was not looking/And I sang my song in a hearable voice: My home, my home, my home." All great songs. Hits.

2 • I would stare at their faces in profile as they sat in my lap in the grass watching the chickens peck for bugs and I believed in everything that they had to offer. I believed and I loved. I loved like I hadn't before. I loved them in a way that was elemental—like water flooding into an empty lagoon in a drought, like a fire to keep you warm in the longest winter, like wind to push your ship through a dead calm. I loved them. Their gentle blue eyes and apple cheeks. Their sparkling minds. Their hope for good times and fair treatment and their

trust in anyone who might come along. I would tell Frankie, "They automatically love and trust everyone they meet. We get that beat right out of us. Why?" "Why" is the question all kids ask. Is the point when we're no longer asking why the point where we start to degrade, to die, to become less than what we once were? A lot of kids I've met are on a stronger, smarter, more deliberate path than most adults. They want to do things, *be* things, and to *know*. They have ideas about the future. Plans. "I want to be a great artist," Frankie's eldest told me when he was five. Good, why not, perfect. At some point life kicks the hell out of us and we stop asking why. As a kid it's hard to imagine anyone would want to hurt you, take advantage of you, lie to you. Until they do, and you're not the same again. How do you live in the world of humanity and still trust humans?

3 • One of my greatest fears is that Frankie's boys won't remember their early days with me as they grow older. If they forget me some fundamental part of myself will be gone forever. I know Frankie's youngest has no true memories of living on the farm. He remembers visits. But those first three years of his life? Those sweet times before it all went to shit? I try to push that out of my head, but it stays like a poison thorn and the tissue around it swells up red and shiny and hard. All our time together here on the farm, forgotten—every good day and every story I read aloud at bedtime ...

4 • It staggers me. I go to a bad place when I think of it and when I go to that place I stay awhile.

5 • In Boulder, Colorado we sit at a dark booth in a downstairs bar where the air smells like a cellar and we drink tequila sunrises. The tequila sunrise is my drink for the summer—tequila, orange juice, grenadine, a cherry as garnish—Luxardo if they have them. At the table it's Alison and me, Ethan and So-hyun, and Kenny Nathaniel. Kenny looks like a young Elijah Wood if Elijah Wood were a punk rock country kid. He's taller and stronger than me, but he carries it easy. Kenny is relaxed. Kenny doesn't care. Kenny smiles and wears a George Strait t-shirt, a camo ball-cap, and his mustache either tells people, "Hey, I'm fun," or "Don't fuck with me even if I *am* fun." I don't think Kenny would hurt a soul, but he's the sort of guy who won't think twice about running straight for trouble.

6 • Kenny sips his tequila sunrise and says, "James my friend, I think this is the drink of our trip," and it's official. Tomorrow Kenny and I hit the road for a summer book tour. We're reading at houses, art galleries, in basements, at parties and infoshops. Kenny has a new book coming out. It's a book a redeemed gunslinger would write. It's beautiful and smart and hilarious and I imagine it must terrify his family.

7 • To paraphrase Bob Dylan, Kenny lives outside the law and he's honest. We all struggle to make our way, but some of us make it look fun. That's Kenny—fun and trouble.

8 • I've always wanted to be an outlaw, but I'm horrified of getting caught. Even a bad test grade in school would send me into fits of awful guilt and I couldn't race home fast enough

to confess to my parents. "I got an F! I'm so *sorry*!" Alison will take a grape or a cherry from a bag in the grocery store to try them out and I have to walk away I'm so afraid of doing something wrong. It's not because I'm moral. The truth is I'm afraid of confrontation. I was one of the small kids in school. I hid from bullies. I don't like answering the phone, setting up doctor's appointments, talking to strangers, arguing about anything, returning things in stores. I'm not an outlaw—I worry too much, and too often.

9 • Growing up in San Diego all my friends were outlaws. Chente Ramirez—living in his car down by Rose Creek, starting fights, pulling knives on people, smashing up parties and bars. Joey Carr—methhead, petty criminal, lost soul. Ben Frank—the king of the shoplifters, expert forger of Greyhound Ameripasses. Agnes McCanty—trainkid, vandal, squatter. Nate Houck—wildcat, destroyer of all things destroyable. Ted Boone—scam artist, drugdealer, con man. My ex Julia—car thief, brawler, acidhead. Julia, who beat up her stepmom and spent a year in jail as a teenager, sharing a cell with a famous double murderer. Me—the goody two shoes, the baby, the wimp, the shy and boring stick-in-the-mud. Sometimes I was so cautious it was as if I'd rendered myself invisible.

10 • Fortune may favor the bold but so does the average person. We like the wild ones, the loud talkers, the brash, the dangerous. Most people are disinterested in the lives of the meek. This says something about the priorities of our culture. The bold, lawless, and brave aren't always the greatest people. Often the quiet ones give you the best things. Kenny is a bit of both—a brilliant, thoughtful, well-read outlaw.

11 • Kenny is part of the new Old West—those who understand the American nightmare and fight each day to wake up from it. They travel hard and hustle and opt out of the terrors of capitalism. His stories are about hitchhiking and trainhoppers, country music, crime of all sorts. He writes from experience, from a place of authority. He's not hiding inside chipping away at some tepid, gutless MFA novel. He's in a pickup truck cracking open a beer after a weird, hilarious catastrophe in the desert. He's riding in the cabs of big rigs, lost in unfamiliar territory, an ear full of strange dialect. So, what does it mean to live outside the law? Is it fine to break laws if you're not hurting anyone? Kenny doesn't hurt anyone. He lives in vans with no registration and at wolf sanctuaries in the wild and sometimes he's back in the city or off in some squat. He likes drugs—mescaline, peyote, mushrooms, cocaine. He shoplifts, loves a good scam. He's an outlaw like Waylon Jennings was an outlaw, like Willie Nelson, heroic, goodhearted—an outlaw whose acts of lawlessness are either celebratory or therapeutic (if he hurts anyone it's himself).

12 • In the late-afternoon sunshine I sit by Boulder Creek with my feet in the cold water while Alison tells Kenny about the drive here from Kansas.

13 • The rapids downstream from us are loud, but they're the kind of loud that loosens you up, the kind that wrings out the knots in your shoulders. Alison sits on the rock higher up from me sipping a black and red can of beer with some sort of death metal logo featuring an arch of goat skulls and a bunch of angry, intense wizards. Kenny stands waist deep in the creek, arms crossed over his chest because even as hot as

it is you don't warm up in mountain spring water.

14 • I move my feet in a figure-8 in the water and I see the creek bottom, dark brown and gold and pebbly, the water moving fast.

15 • The air smells like pine—tangy, the smell of sap. It smells like drying rocks, weed someone's smoking under the bridge upstream, and reedy creek water. It's a glorious day in Colorado. I shut my eyes and see the image of a dusty mason jar full of cat's eye marbles sitting on a windowsill then lightning spidering across a black skyline, a camel standing up slowly with someone on its back, a mushroom cloud in the sea expanding outward. Eyes closed—my head's a wildly cycling mess; I can't hold a thought in place. Eyes open—it tightens back to focus and I'm there in the present. Eyes closed—a dragon sleeping on a pile of gold, TV static in a dark room and then the screen goes off and the room is black. Eyes open—us here, this place here, the things Alison is talking about. Left to my own devices I'm a hurricane; I'm a stuttering, jittering, shambled catastrophe. Eyes open—

16 • —eyes open, Alison tells Kenny how the night before we stayed at the High Plains Campground in western Kansas and walked right into a wedding reception in the bar. "The place was beat the fuck *up*," she says. "Last time James and I were there they had a mini golf course out back, but now it's all weeds and cracked concrete and they've got a couple goats and a bunch … like, a bunch of stray cats hangin' out around the old cement castles and fairy tale statues. So, we go … we walk

in and it's all these crusty ol' bikers and their wives. We're the youngest people in there by, what, 20, 30 years?" "About." "Yeah, about, and they're having a wedding reception, which consists of ... there's a grocery store sheet cake and the groom ... this ol' cowboy hat wearing, leather vest, potbellied, gray-bearded biker in yellow aviator glasses ... he's hosting karaoke for everybody with his laptop set up on the pool table. We sit down at a booth and order some beers."

17 • We sit down at a booth and order some beers. Alison and I across from each other holding hands over the tabletop. The karaoke host groom sings "Luckenbach, Texas," and I sing along under my breath, then louder as Alison smiles at me, her eyes sparkling with the lights behind the karaoke station. The waitress sets a couple pint glasses of beer on the table (spilling mine, but I don't care) and asks if we want food. "I'm so hungry I could eat that pool table!" Alison says. The waitress laughs, "Y'want fries with that, babe?" We order deep-fried pickles, onion rings, steak fries, and two more beers. "Y'got it, kids." The waitress walks back to the bar, dancing a little to the song the karaoke host is singing. "I like being kids," Alison says. "Yeah, totally," I say, "tonight we're kids." "Hey, man," says a biker lady at the next table with white hair dyed pink on the ends and pulled back in a ponytail, "Y'gotta git up there 'n' sang. Y'gotta sang! Yer next!" I tell her I can't sing, and she says, "Ohhh, yer inna band I can tell. I know y'can sang. I cain't wait." "Maybe after some more beers," I nod down at my glass. "Oh, no, yer next. Y'gotta git up there. Doan lemme down, kid!"

18 • After the bartender does David Allan Coe's "You Never Even Called Me by My Name" and the bride and groom duet on Kid Rock and Sheryl Crow's "Picture," I get up the courage and sing the Willie and Merle version of Townes Van Zandt's "Pancho and Lefty," standing next to the groom who scrolls through song-titles on his laptop screen as I sing, the blue and white text moving in reflection on the lenses of his glasses. When I'm done I hand him the mic and tell him I've never done this before and he tells me not to worry, it's all just for fun.

19 • A few songs and two beers later I stand next to him and sing Hank Jr's "Family Tradition" while Alison sits at our table eating a slice of wedding cake on a paper plate with a white plastic fork. I close my eyes tight when I know a few lines by heart and I sing loud and sure, my stomach going sour when my voice cracks. It was great.

20 • "It was great," Alison tells Kenny. "The next morning we woke up to endless rolling prairie behind our tent and *horses* off in the field and the biggest blue sky. It's a special place. Just this weird, old, half-ruined, savage prairie outpost. It's like 20 bucks to stay there. You'd love it." "I bet." Kenny lets himself sink up to his chin in the creek water. He takes a big breath and then he goes under and his camo hat floats away. He breaks through the surface with a gasp and swims a few strokes to fetch his hat and pulls it back on. "You guys gotta come *in*," he tells us as he climbs out onto the rocks, "It'll wake you up."

21 • I lower myself off the rock I'm sitting on then plunge in and swim awkwardly to the middle of the creek against the current, thrashing my arms and kicking my legs to stay warm. My heart seizures to life and thumps hard in my chest and my lungs ache and then I'm warm. I turn over on my back and float downstream to where Alison and Kenny are sitting on the rocks, the white tips of my feet sticking out of the dark water in front of me.

22 • That night in Ethan's spare room in Denver I lie in bed while Alison sleeps next to me and I write my exit note in my head. I tell people I'm done and that I can't do this anymore and please don't contact me because I'm throwing out my phone and deleting my email address and moving away and I'll never see you guys again. I write this note like I've always written this note on so many sleepless nights when I've given up and plan to cut myself off from the outside world. The sun comes up while I'm still removing myself and then the room is light and when I see that it's morning I know I've got a dread I won't shake for a while. I go through my lists of reasons and none are strong enough to keep me from quitting. When I hear Ethan and So-Hyun stirring I close my eyes and pretend to sleep. I hear the glass patio door slide open. I hear a coffee grinder. The shower turning on. At some point I sleep, but a lawnmower kicks to life outside and wakes me up again. I sit up in bed and look out the window. Behind Ethan's house you can see the Rockies, dim and hazy gray against the pale blue sky.

23 • Frankie's boys are with their dad in Portland all summer. It's the first summer of their lives I haven't seen them. I do the

math and I realize it's been a full year since we were together last. They spent two weeks in Kansas last summer. We had breakfast at the Waffle House down on 7, walked along the creek, dug trenches and waterways in the sand at the Clinton Lake swim beach, played with Star Wars figures, built Lego spaceships, swam in a kiddie pool Alison picked up at Target. At the Wyandotte County Fair we watched the piglet races, rode the Ferris wheel in the dusk, ate blue and pink cotton candy and drank strawberry lemonade. We threw darts at balloons to win stuffed animals, ran through the fun house past the woozing mirrors and across the shifting floor plates. We fed the camel and a wild-eyed ostrich at the petting zoo and watched a giant tortoise with a grim, ancient face move as slow as paint dripping down a wall. At some point both the ostrich and the camel grabbed Frankie's eldest's black and white trucker cap off his head and in a photo he's grinning ecstatically next to the ostrich holding his crumpled hat in its dinosaur beak. I think about that as Kenny and I drive east through pine woods, past farmhouses tucked back in the green rolling hills and lakes with sky blue water reflecting the clouds, past road construction and semi trucks full of cows bound for slaughter.

24 • I drive and Kenny messes with the radio. It's all Mexican stations out here and we stop at one where the song is fast and loose and jittery, a cumbia track with shakers, handclaps, and horns over electronic beats. "*This* song!" shouts Kenny. He sings along in Spanish as he eats Doritos from a family-size bag in his lap. We nod our heads and look at each other and laugh as he and the singer sing: "*Cuando bailas yo bailo/cuando bailo tu bailas/soy feo feo feo pero bailo bailo bailo.*" Kenny laughs and says, "Dude, I love this song. The singer is like,

'I'm ugly ugly ugly, but I dance dance dance.' It's not 'I'm ugly, but I *can* dance' like you might think. It's 'I'm ugly, *but* I dance.' Fucking awesome. I love cumbia. It's weirdo music for weirdos." "Do you think he's actually ugly?" I ask. "Oh, probably not." "I hope he's ugly," I say, "I want him to be ugly for the sake of the song." "I think he's probably pretty cute," Kenny says thoughtfully, "He's got a cute voice. Or maybe he *thinks* he's ugly, but everyone knows he's not. Like the star of a high school makeover movie where they just fix their hair and take off their glasses and everyone sees they're hot, but at the end of the movie it doesn't matter because it's what's inside that counts."

25 • I stare out the window at a big red Ford truck pulling past us. The sticker on the back window of the Ford is an old comic strip character—a little blonde boy wearing a cowboy hat, grinning wickedly over his shoulder as he urinates onto the words "City Boys."

26 • "Calvin pissing on city boys!" shouts Kenny happily.

27 • Passing by a pond in a green field with black cattle standing around it—some of them with faces down to the water, drinking.

28 • Passing by an abandoned barn—gray slat boards, a collapsing roof, tall grass, rain clouds in the humid air.

29 • Passing by a billboard with "JESUS IS WATCHING" in tall white letters against a black background.

30 • We pass the Ford an hour later and laugh about the Calvin sticker again. In my lap my phone starts to buzz, and I grab it and flip it over. It's a text from Frankie's eight-year-old. He and his brother have a phone now so Frankie can check in on them while they're at their dad's. It's a gif, an image of him wearing a plastic Roman soldier helmet, holding the lid of a Rubbermaid tub as a shield and wielding what looks like a rolled-up poster as a sword. He's shirtless like he and his brother often are, and he has his bottom lip jutted out, frowning in a way that's meant to look tough, but I can tell he's trying not to laugh. The photo zooms in on a loop through a series of close-ups, a full body shot, then closer, his head tilting to the side a little, then a full close-up of just his face and his trying-not-to-laugh tough expression. When I look at the photo the dread in my chest is gone. I text back, "Haha! I love this!" and wait for a response. There's none, but I feel the lightness wash over me and it stays.

31 • In the morning hungover, we drive down the main strip of the town from last night's tour-stop. It has redbrick storefronts locked up with metal accordion gates because it's a Sunday, wet blacktop beginning to steam, a pink adobe church with a crowd of people filing in and a group of children in little kid suits and puffy dresses running wild on the grass lawn. A block down from that is a shop selling fancy clothes for *quinceañeras*, Stetson hats, and colorful slim-cut cowboy suits, then a *carniceria*, a *panaderia*, and a gas station with no one at the pumps but a brown and white

dog sniffing the squeegee bin (then lifting his leg to piss).

32 • "There," Kenny points as I drive. "There. Right there. Boom. Taqueria Los Panchos #4. *That's* our breakfast."

33 • Inside, Kenny orders for us in Spanish and we sit down at a booth with a TV mounted on the wall above us playing a *telenovela*, the sound off. "*Uno cuatro cinco?* One four five?" It's our order. I get up and grab it for us. Two burritos, yellow-paper-wrapped on a red plastic tray. Chicken quesadilla in a styrofoam box for Kenny. Side of hot carrots for me on a small paper plate with a few slices of lime. "Oh my *god* this looks fucking awesome," says Kenny. I ask him to explain his burrito because I like hearing people talk about their food. He takes a bite and says, "Carnitas burrito. Shreds of pork with—" taking another bite "—with some kind of ... some kind of *lime* sauce and beans, *really* good beans ... onions and peppers cooked down to muck but in a good way. James my friend, this is perfect, the perfect thing for right now, the only thing you could ever want in a moment like *right now*. If this burrito were running for president I'd vote for it and it would win." I pull the paper off mine and take a bite. My burrito has refried beans, lovely soft orange rice, and guacamole, the tortilla cooked to a tawny gold with brown spots and dusty with flour. Before the next bite I squeeze lime into the open end of the burrito, a bit of the juice flicking onto my chin and then my nose is full of the smell of it.

34 • Tonight we're reading at a bougie, fancy bookstore and we're worried about it. The place is called Edgemont Street

Books, but we've taken to calling it Edgemont Street Crooks to prepare ourselves for the disappointment of no one showing. The parties and bars and house shows are good to us. The rowdy crowds, dumpstered potlucks, Black Lives Matter and ACAB posters on the walls, spilled beer on the stage, no stage at all, noise bands playing after the readers, drunken country music karaoke afterward, yes, all good. Clean, well-stocked bookstores with the latest celebrity memoirs, a novelty gift section bigger than most independent shops, and inspirational posters with beach scenes, mountain climbers, and sunsets, not so much. Edgemont Street Crooks. Drudgemont Street Pukes.

35 • My paranoid hangover brain tells me tonight will be a disaster, tonight will be shit, it will be embarrassing, no one will come, anyone who *does* come won't like us, will think we're dirty, will laugh at our ratty country punk clothes.

36 • Kenny comes back from the counter with a takeout cup of *horchata*, sips it, and says, "Are we really doing this? Edgemont Meat Hooks?" I laugh and say, "They're gonna lock the doors and murder us afterward." Kenny says, "A little bird told me Edgemont Street is where all the cannibals in town hang out. Maybe they're luring us in to eat us." "A little bird told *me* that when the readings are over they tie the writers to a tree outside and beat the hell out of them with sticks. Which is pretty cool I guess and now I kind of like them." He shakes a finger for emphasis and says, "A little bird told me this is going to be fucking dumb and *we're* fucking dumb for even *doing* this." We laugh. "This is going to be an absolute shitshow." "Abso*lute*."

37 • I wrap the last three inches of my burrito in its yellow paper and look up at the TV screen behind Kenny. A tall man with silver-streaked hair in a dark gray suit stands at the side of a swimming pool at night, the water bright blue, its warbly refraction dancing across the stone wall behind him with the shimmering pool lights. The man stares off into the night— stern, regal, wizened. The mansion behind him is lit up with a spray of golden windows.

38 • That night after the reading we're in a country bar down by the river and the bartender is buying our drinks. Why, we're not sure, but it's tequila sunrise after tequila sunrise and I've fed ten bucks into the jukebox to play every version of "Carmelita" in a row then every Townes song they've got. I'm giving Kenny a list of ways I might die on this book tour that have to be kept a secret for PR reasons. "If I die on the toilet for any reason you can't tell anyone." He laughs and says, "I'll tell them you died fighting *narcos*." "Good. If I die by slipping on the bathroom floor and hitting my head, the same." "Right, bathroom deaths. *Check*. Any and all bathroom deaths I'll tell them it was *narcos*." "Tell them El Chapo got out of jail and I had to fight him mid-tour to save all the children and all the baby animals in the world. Even the snakes." "Even the snakes," he says raising his glass in salute. "But the *baby* snakes," I say, "The horrifying baby snakes but they're babies too so they make the cut." "What about the grownup snakes?" "*Not* on the guest list," I slam my fist onto the bar top for emphasis. "No plus-one for grownup snakes," he says. "No plus-one and *no* drink tickets. Don't even ask, you sneaky long pretending-to-be-a-rope-then-scaring-people bastards. Stay outside! You're 86'd, motherfuckers." "What are we even *talking* about?" he says laughing, shaking his head.

39 • "Alright then, what is a good death?" Kenny asks as the bartender sets another on-the-house round in front of us. "Well, I guess being killed by lions. Killed by alligators. Saving people from fires. Killing Hitler because I've traveled back in time to right the wrongs of history. Dying while being a cool surfing bank robber like *Point Break*. Fighting grownup snakes. Fighting evil vampires but where I'm a good vampire like Wesley Snipes and I have two swords I drag on the ground as I walk toward my enemies and I get to wear stupid looking '90s sunglasses and a big black coat. Oh, and definitely fighting wicked space aliens." "If you're killed by wicked aliens I'll tell them you were killed by wicked aliens because that's fuckin' legit and epic. Take that, you space-age bastards!" "Good, Kenny, thank you. Being killed by a wicked space-age bastard is legit and epic and an all-around good death and anyone should be proud to die like that. What else? Eaten by a buncha crazy-ass dinosaurs. You can tell the truth if that happens. And of course fighting *narcos*. Always tell the truth about me fighting *narcos* if I end up fighting *narcos*, and I will do the same for you. I think I saw some *narcos* outside the bar walking a couple dogs so be careful." I make these jokes to shove the real stuff away. The car accidents and viruses and cancer, the heart attacks, the bleak and unromantic scenes that play out in my head on a stuttering loop most days. The scenes that come rushing in after my brain tells me *But you will DIE someday* apropos of nothing.

40 • *But you will DIE someday.* How often have I thought those words? In so many houses, bedrooms, restaurants, cars, buses, fields, classrooms, bathtubs, airplanes, trains, on so many sidewalks, at parties, in bars, alone or with friends, up late at night or in the clear light of dawn. The words loop, they get louder as they repeat, they come in rolling orbit, a circular

course, a churning wheel. *But you will die someday. But you will DIE someday. BUT YOU WILL DIE SOMEDAY.*

41 • How many times will I think those words before my day comes?

42 • What good does it do for me to think them?

43 • Nothing. It does no good at all.

44 • None at all. Right now I am alive and being alive is so much better than the alternative I'm sent into waves of euphoria. Tonight I'm going to drink a tequila sunrise big enough to put out a California wildfire. I'm going to be joyous with my joyful friend. I'm going to lasso the sun like Pecos Bill and pull it toward me. C'mere you solar bastard, I am bringing forever summer! Hello sweet bartender, get me another. Get me a dozen and I'll shout, "Don't go nowhere!" as loud as a jet engine and get the words tattooed on my face. I'll feed another ten bucks into the jukebox and play every version of "Carmelita" and every Townes song AGAIN.

45 • *But you will DIE someday.* Not today I won't.

46 • We drink a toast to the Edgemont Street Crooks. "To the Edgemont Street Crooks!" "To goddamn fuckin' *Edgemont!*"

"What an utter shit-show." "*What* a shit-show."

47 • We drink a toast to the dawning glory of the tequila sunrise.

48 • We drink a toast to the bartender and stickers of Calvin pissing and space-age bastards. We drink a toast to Taqueria Los Panchos #4, to country music and tomorrow morning's breakfast and to every breakfast after that. At some point I get half the bar to shout, "Lakeside Speed Waaaayne!" ten times and it feels like an invocation—an exorcism of the bland and a salute to the chaotic powers that rule and turn the Earth.

49 • Around closing time *we're* the *narcos* and I pull my merch table cash out of my pocket and shake it in the air, "We're *narcos*! I want to kill!" I yell. "*Quiero matar! Quiero morir!*" Kenny shouts. I get on my knees on the wooden stool and shout across the crowded bar, "*Somos narcos* and I will fight any bastard in this bar!" I don't want to fight any bastard anywhere, but I'm happy and stupid with my friend and we care about nothing but the next tequila sunrise and jukebox country songs and yelling about how we're *narcos*. Kenny says, "*Somos narcos* and we will *fight* our way out of trouble." I shake my $40 in ones in the air again and say, "*No tengo miedo* anymore! *Somos narcos ricos!*" Kenny laughs, shaking his head, and says, "Holy shit let's go before they throw us out." "No, they love us here. Someone just told me we're the new owners. Hey! Hey everybody! Quiet down! Listen up! We own this place! Hey! Drinks are free tonight! We love you! Who loves you?! *We* love you! Batman's a piece of shit!" Kenny half chokes on his drink and says, "Dude, what, James,

why did you say Batman's a piece of shit?" "I don't know! I have no real opinion about Batman. Just seemed like the right thing to say." "Fuck you, Batman!" shouts Kenny, raising his drink in the air. "Batman you are *trash*! Go home!" I yell, giving double middle fingers to the ceiling. "Go home, you're drunk, Batman!" yells Kenny.

50 • The edges blur. The features blur. Someone drops a glass and I hear it shatter on the floor. Fighting against the slur in my mouth, I tell Kenny, "Lesh gih outta here 'fore we fight ever'one in here." "Less figh evereee'one in here and *thhhen* gih owwa here," he says tapping his forehead wisely. The bartender sets two more free drinks in front of us. The tall glasses are bright yellow at the top and then red at the bottom—a deep, murmuring cloud of red like the blood in an egg yolk. Kenny climbs off his bar stool and walks toward the restrooms, staggering a little to the left. Someone high-fives him and he accepts this gladly. I see the bartender pull the tap down and fill a pint glass with golden beer.

51 • Back on the farm two weeks later Alison and I sit on the couch and watch an Italian-made Western movie from the '70s. Honeybee, the gray tabby kitten we found hiding in the barn a few days ago, lies curled up asleep on the blanket covering my lap, her soft little paws wrapped around her face to block out the light. As I pet her, Honeybee begins to twitch, dreaming. She groans a kitten "Mmrrrr" in her sleep then settles back into the blanket. "She was dreaming a kitten dream," I say. Alison pets her tiny head with one finger and says, "Oh little *thing*." The film is about a vaquero carrying a wooden chest across the desert tied behind his saddle. What's in the chest

the movie never says, but he protects it from Union soldiers and federales and Texas Rangers. He holds it over his head as he rides across a swelling creek during a midnight rainstorm. "It's raining in the movie and it's raining here," I say. "Maybe *we're* the movie and *he's* real," she nods at the screen. "Probably," I say pretending to be serious. "Definitely," she says even more serious than me. Outside the farmhouse, a storm is lashing the windows. Thunder cracks hard and sharp and we both jump a little and the dogs in the next room begin to bark and whine. "Whoa, it's gettin' *close*," says Alison as the dark room flashes bright as day with lightning. We put the movie on pause so Alison can make popcorn.

52 • The popcorn Alison likes to make is cooked in olive oil and seasoned with salt and pepper and nutritional yeast. (Popcorn is something we've always got on hand, even during the lean months when the fridge gets bare. Tonight she'll add fresh rosemary from the garden.) While it pops I put on a country record made by a guy my age. The song I play is full of soaring pedal steel that aches right into you. It's about heartache, infidelity, new love—about checking in with an old lover and wanting the best for them. I played it for Alison the week we got together and she cried and told me she wasn't ready. Sometimes art hurts so much you want to look away no matter how good it is. You want to bury that book at the bottom of your laundry hamper. You want to drop that record off at Goodwill or break it over your knee like an angry cartoon character. It's well done and it's true, but it hurts and sometimes that drives you away. When the popcorn is done Alison dumps it from the pot into a big glass bowl and we sit back down on the couch. I hit Play and the paused scene jumps to life.

53 • The vaquero is sitting next to a campfire at night, eating beef stew from a small tin bowl. The sparks rise to the moon— the moon a white fingernail sliver. He sits back with his bedroll behind him and he stares up at the sky. The stars hang speckled and vast above him. He's alone and he has always been alone. You know this. You knew this coming into the film, but it still hurts. He pulls a tattered paperback from his pack and opens it to the middle and begins to read.

54 • As we finish the popcorn, the vaquero rides slow through the desert in the heat of the day—weary, sweat-soaked, leg and shoulder dark with blood, nodding off in his saddle, head bowed. He's beat to hell, shot twice, but he's got away from the men following him and you know he'll make it out of this. He's the hero. He's safe. He'll die like us all, but the movie will end before that happens. Behind him the wooden chest sways side to side, still tied down, but one of the ropes has come undone and it drags in the dust at the feet of the horse. The music is a tremendous swell of symphony strings, an orchestra full of ache and grandeur, tension then relief, a Spanish guitar strummed just above it all to remind us we're in the West. The credits roll.

PART
FOUR

Autumn, 2019

1 • I'm in California on a short book tour when Alison texts to tell me our landlord has sold the farm out from under us. All summer he's fixed things without asking. The busted water pump in the basement. The patchy clapboard. The broken window in the front room. At the beginning of September he hired a crew to paint the farmhouse a lovely white and navy blue and rebuild all the damaged window sills. We felt lucky and thought nothing of it and spoke highly of him. Then the text: "Rustin sold the house to his son-in-law. He just told me. We have two months to get out." "Two months is Christmas." "I know. I asked if we could push the date back, but he hasn't got back to me." "He can't kick us out at Christmas." "He is."

2 • October on the farm is sad and quiet and hard. Given an extension until February to find a new place, we spend hours each day looking at listings. Because no one rents out rural properties in our area we're forced to buy. We get a quote—a low-income loan from a lender in town. It's not much, but it's enough to get a few acres and a small farmhouse we could fix up ourselves. To move the farm and not get rid of the animals we'll need at least three acres safe for agricultural use and some sort of out-building to put them up for the night. It's slim pickings. Our real estate agent Alexis tells us most people don't list properties during the holidays. "You'll see a bunch of new ones pop up in January. People don't want to hassle it during Christmas." "We have to be out by February." "Yeaaah, I know, I know. I'll tell you when it's time to panic."

3 • We panic.

4 • We keep looking.

5 • The grass in the field dies and then it's a pale, wind-swept yellow where there was once lush green. The trees turn in the middle of October and overnight their leaves are gone. Alison and I carve pumpkins that rot a week later and Halloween passes by with no memory of what we did.

6 • The days grow shorter, colder. Thanksgiving is at a family farm a few miles from ours and entirely forgettable.

7 • The first snow of the year comes one night at the end of November. The next morning the fields are smooth and white, the sun sparkling diamonds across the snow drifts, a blue glow at dusk with the long shadows of the trees stretching out to the road. We make an offer on a beautiful decaying farmhouse in Weston and are promptly out-bid. Alexis says, "Don't worry, you guys. We have time. I got you. We're good." We make an offer on a miserable ruin in Tonganoxie and suffer the same fate. We meet up with Alexis every couple of days. She leads us through derelict trailers on two-acre scrub plots, into farmhouses we fall in love with that are promptly sold to someone else that very day. Alexis—tall, blonde, with stylish nerd glasses, a smoker's cough, and a ballerina ponytail—tells us that this is all part of buying a home. "We've kind of fucked ourselves," Alison says as we stand in front of an old colonial country manor gone to seed, "We need rural land, but we have to be close to my job and we want to be away from neighbors. Also, we don't make enough money for what we want." "Yeah, you've fucked yourselves, but we'll keep looking. I don't want

you guys to settle for something you don't love and end up hating me." We crunch through the snow and climb up the creaking porch steps of the colonial. Alexis knocks, pushing the door where the handle would be were this not a ruin. The door swings open, creaking loose on its hinges. "Real estate agent!" she shouts into the gloomy parlor.

8 • Alexis and Alison love the fixer-uppers. They see the potential and say things like, "Oh, this one has good bones" when I'm horrified at the trash piles left in backfields and the mold spots from water damage speckling the ceiling. I'm afraid of getting something that will suck up all our resources. We don't have the money for most of these places, even the shitholes. All I see are the worst-case scenarios, the hard times when people stop buying books, the peaks and valleys. Alexis and Alison are braver than me. They're fine with the gamble, with the bold leap. I'm pushed to hide inside with all my fear and self-doubt crushing me; they're pushing for the future. I can't trick myself to believe the future even *exists*. I've always surrounded myself with capable, decisive people because I'm not one of them. Maybe it's a self-preservative measure, a matter of finding the right social chemistry in the name of survival. I can hustle to get my books read by people. I can place trust in the potential of my work, because while I don't think my writing is worth a damn yet, I truly believe that someday I'll write something that will matter. That "someday" is all I need to get through the hours and keep working. If I were to pick myself apart I'm sure I'd find layers of delusion that would suck the wind from my sails. In order to get out of bed each morning, I choose to believe and not look overly hard or close at the substantiality and utility of my belief.

9 • A friend, a devout Catholic, once told me, "Everyone worships something. Even atheists worship. They worship *themselves*. We're spiritual by nature even if we don't know we're spiritual." Maybe I worship the potential to do great work one day, the belief that I *have it in me*, that if I just keep working, keep believing, I'll find my way to something true and sound and lasting. I think of Augustine's *Confessions*. His path toward spiritual conversion, the years he spent wanting to believe and knowing one day he *would* believe, but there was always something that kept him from taking the next step. Inside, where it counts, we're all boats tossed on stormy seas. We're all a shitty, caterwauling mess when you break out that magnifying glass. I can't judge anyone because I know how hard it is to be human. Look at the most squared-away person you know and I guarantee they'll tell you they're a failure, a wreck of a human, too nervous to live, too weird to succeed. We're all just fighting to make our way. When you think about it like that how could you not love everyone? How could you not forgive everything short of the unforgiveable? We're damaged, battered, scared, repressed, besieged by anxiety, agh, what an awful thing to be human. But what a wonderful thing we are! What a thing to *love*. Do you blame the victim for stumbling through life after they've been hurt or do you set your angry glare upon the aggressor? What if we're all victims? What if everyone is just trying to climb back up to the light after being shoved into a shitty black hole? When you understand that you begin to understand part of what love is—the ability to step back and say, "I'm like this too. We're not so different."

10 • It's hard to have enemies when you appreciate the commonality; when you see that the things you hate about them are often the things you hate about yourself. Maybe we

need to ignore that in order to feel unique. Think of animals. They have personalities for lack of a better word, peculiarities specific to them, but they follow a code, they exist in the patterns you see in all members of their species—at least to some degree, barring aberrations. Humans are the same. Our pattern is *mess*. Our pattern is disaster, self-doubt. It's fish-out-of-water and it's a plane lost in the 'fog. We can fake it beautifully, but no one has any idea what they're doing. Is that comforting, that we're all fucking up together? Today it is. Today it's like a lantern in a storm, a pale and flickering light to trudge toward when all else feels doomed. It's a thought that tells me this: "Don't go nowhere."

11 • The first week of December I'm in an airport bar, an untouched glass of tequila in front of me. It's loud here, the music deafening. There are solitary travelers like myself at tall, round tables with Coronas and Bud Lights. Families at the booths and larger tables along the walls, talking soundlessly or arguing or faces down to their phones and tablets. The woman at the table next to me tells the guy she's with, "I call that *progress*." The guy is Native American. He wears a quilted green snow vest and a long-sleeve white thermal (the sleeves rolled up) and he has a camouflage trucker cap pulled low over his shoulder-length black hair. The girl is young and blonde with twin braids that start at her hairline near her temples and end at her neck. She wears a long gray skirt and a thick white sweater that's maybe angora, but when I think about it I'm not sure what angora is. Wool? Cat hair? (Which sounds gross.) Alpaca? Goat? My mind drifts off and then she says, "Challenge accepted!" and I snap back into focus. He says, "I was really honest with them. You're going to be the first person to know." The conversation falls behind a clatter of dishes from the kitchen and the terrible pop-country music

and the waitress setting a plate of quesadillas down in front of an old woman to my left wearing round, owlish glasses. The waitress says, "Hi again! Beer?" The woman looks up, blinking, confused, the lenses of her glasses catching the light, rendering them opaque, white, silver. The waitress nods at the beer bottle sitting on the table and says, "You okay or do you need another one?"

12 • When I left the farm it was snowing. As a kid I thought that as soon as it was cold that was when winter began. December 1st. It's still fall. Bleak featureless skies and the dark skeletons of trees. Muddy culverts, yellow fields. On the drive to the airport Alison and I talked about the hunt for houses. "Alexis sent me a bunch more listings last night. A couple of them look okay." "Let's go see 'em when I'm back." "One is … it's in Lawrence on five acres, but maybe it's a doublewide? Or a manufactured home? The listing's not clear. Sometimes it's hard to tell. It's HUD, which is a problem." "HUD means it's foreclosed?" "Yeah, it means it's foreclosed." "I don't want to take someone's house. That feels wrong." "James, we're running out of time, and anyway once it's foreclosed it's already taken. I guess no one's lived in this one for ages. It's $145,000 which we can just barely qualify for." "Okay, tell Alexis we'll go see it. Make an appointment for when I'm back." "It *is* Lawrence and that means it's on the up. Also, the comps look really good." The wind knocked against the side of the car and moved us out of our lane. Alison swerved back. "Whoa, the fuckin' *wind*," she said. "I heard it all night," I told her, "We should've brought the cats in." The woods alongside the road were gray. The sky and highway the same drained, blanched color. In the airport bar I'm lonely because airports are lonely and because bars are lonely and even the people sitting here with loved ones look alone. Most stare at their

phones, frowning. They listen to music from white ear buds while the person they're with eats in silence.

13 • The couple sitting to the right of me have bought a house. I've been eavesdropping. "It'll be fine once we paint," he says. The canned voice over the airport PA says, "All passengers ... must have ... proper ID." It sounds dystopic, robotic, cold. I think of the first time I flew alone. I was five, off to see my grandparents at their farm in Colorado and because I was excited to do that I dressed as a cowboy—brown plastic cowboy hat from Susan's Toys, felt vest with a sheriff's badge pinned on, twin die-cast cap guns in holsters dangling off my belt, clapping side to side as I walked to the gate. This was years before 9/11, but Lindbergh Field security took my guns. I was inconsolable. On the plane without the protection of my cap guns I was sure it was going to crash. The guy lifts his burger to his mouth and takes a bite. Still chewing he says, "Yuh know what we gah do? We gah sell thuh couch. ASAP. Hundred bucks. I can try and find some plywood and get those legs on there. We can make it look good." The girl shows him her phone, "I like this, but I don't like the garden." What they say sounds disconnected, as if each one's conversation is not dependent upon the other. "Honestly if we see something let's just put it on my credit card," says the guy, balling up his napkin, dropping it on his unfinished burger, pushing the plate away from him. "Ugh, I'm stuffed," he says, rubbing his belly up and down.

14 • I feel alone in the airport bar and the snow is falling outside as seen from the big wall-length windows behind the check-in counters at the gate and I see an uncertain future,

time stretching out in front of us without a sure thing to grab onto. We know that change will come, but we think that this change will always be good. We're rarely prepared when the bad sort hits. The girl says, "This is way too much emotion for me." The guy gets up to walk to the restroom, stopping to bend down and kiss the top of her head then smoothing her hair as he goes. When he's gone she puts down her phone and picks up his and scrolls through it. I look away because it feels wrong to be witnessing this, whatever this is. When I look up again the waitress is standing at their table. She points to the girl's beer without saying anything. The girl says, "I'm gonna do one more" and sets the man's phone back in its place.

15 • Forty-eight hours later I'm in a new airport bar, a new city. It was snowing this morning when I woke up. I stood at the window and pulled the orange and brown motel curtain open and saw gray sky and rows of parked cars and the snow falling. The boys were still asleep. Frankie's seven-year-old, Johnsy, slept outside the blankets in just his blue and red underwear with his arm around his brother Willy, who lay wrapped like a burrito with the covers. I flew in yesterday and Jude, their dad, Frankie's ex, met me at the motel and handed them off. Jude walked us down the paisley carpeted hallway to the room and I told him it was good to see him, that he looked healthy. "Sometimes it feels like a year, sometimes fifty," he said as the boys unpacked their bags on the bed by the window. "I hear that. Thanks for bringing them by." The room smelled just vaguely of cigarettes and bleach. "Yeah, course, wish I would've known earlier. Could've given you more time." "It's super last minute. I'm just happy to be here." "Alright, boys ... hey guys, come hug your dad goodbye." They ran to him and hugged his knees. "Be super good for James, okay?" "Yeah!" "We will!" "Alright, you guys have a great

time!" "Thanks, Jude. Thank you." "Yeah, for sure." Jude shut the door and I took off my coat and dropped it on the bed by the window. "Alright, guys. Sooo, since I'm missing Willy's birthday ... and because Christmas is a few weeks away ... I figured we would—" I walked over to my suitcase on the bed and unzipped it. They ran to it, waiting, looking up at me, smiling. "—I figured we would do Christmas and Willy's birthday early!" Johnsy began to jump up and down, clapping his hands. "Yes! Please! Yes!" I pulled the lid off the suitcase and showed them the wrapped presents I'd brought. "Yes, yes, yes!" said Willy. He wrapped his arms around my waist and his legs around my leg. "Okay, ow, okay, you're getting too big for that ... you're... ooh, ow, jump off." Willy detached himself and climbed up on the bed. "Can we jump on the bed?!" "Of course!" Johnsy joined him and they bounced, leaping from bed to bed, jumping then letting themselves fall cross-legged back onto the mattress. "Sound like a good plan? Early birthday? Early Christmas?" "Yes!" shouted Willy. "Yes!" shouted Johnsy.

16 • In the airport bar I get a text from Willy. "We're home now." Earlier I'd asked him to let me know when they were safe and sound. I text him, "I'm so sad to leave." "Me too." "I need more Willy and Johnsy time." "I need more James time." After that he texts me a series of sad emojis—a row of yellow faces, mouths open, twin fountains of tears bursting from their eyes, a frowning cat, a sad dog, a depressed looking pig, and then more yellow faces. In the bar I order my second double tequila. There are TV screens everywhere you look. Some playing sports and reality makeover shows, others pop-country music videos disconnected from the awful beachy, white boy reggae song over the speakers about how amber is the color of someone's energy.

17 • The boys and I spent our time building a Lego model of a scene from *Avengers: Infinity War*, eating all-day breakfast twice daily at the Big Boy next to the motel, discussing the moral alignment of the clone troopers from Star Wars, and talking about Pokémon. I know nothing about Pokémon, but when they love something I love it too. I listen to anything they want to tell me about. I'm excited for whatever they're excited about even if it means nothing to me. I think that's part of what love is. You love someone so much that whatever they're interested in dazzles you. Doesn't matter what it is— you believe in them and because of that you believe in the things they believe. Sometimes love is about setting yourself aside and becoming the other person for a while because you can't imagine a better thing than them. You love the things they love because you love the person they are and anything that's a part of them has new import.

18 • The boys and I went to bed late. They struggled against bedtime and sat up straight in bed at any sound and tortured each other and squealed with laughter and made endless appeals to play longer or have one last piece of the reindeer-shaped Christmas chocolate I brought. And then, like a switch flicked off, they were asleep and I could finally look at them. I could look at them because when they're awake they move so fast it's like trying to see a hummingbird's wings or a bullet fired from a gun. I love that part of them, but this was good too. I sat up in bed and watched them sleep and everything felt precarious and fleeting and perfectly right. It was the same feeling I get on long sleepless nights when *But you will DIE someday* comes to fight me and after hours of struggling with it I realize tonight I'm alive and that no matter what I'm going through being alive is fantastically better than the alternative. When that happens I feel the beauty and

glory of life. That sort of joy is restorative and invigorating. It disregards as inconsequential whatever dark things you're dealing with and fills you with a relief and excitement that's almost breathless. It's the only time I feel as if I'm truly living in the present moment. That reminder of death reminds you instead of *life*. Life! I am alive! I am here and there are things I'm going to do and those things are going to feel remarkably good! The world is full of those good things if you can see it with the right kind of eyes—just look! Roll that stone aside and see what's underneath. Shine your flashlight up into the trees. Sweep aside the fog from the window glass. Stare into the darkness until you *see*! Sitting up late as the boys slept and knowing we'd have a morning together in just a few hours was the same feeling. When you're able to think this way it makes you appreciate what is before you and gives you a strength and courage that is unlike anything else.

19 • Sitting up late as the boys slept, I looked at them and I thought, *Don't go nowhere. PLEASE.*

20 • In the airport bar it's a Christmas song about how last Christmas the singer gave someone his heart and the very next day whomever it was gave it away, but this year he'll give it to someone special. An older woman sits slumped forward at the bar in a Santa Claus hat, eating tortilla chips and queso dip, and playing solitaire on her phone. In front of her, the bartender wipes the counter with a white rag and neither sees the other. It's snowing harder outside. The planes sit next to the gates with white flakes gusting around them and the sky is colorless. Flights are canceled and delayed. People stand in long lines at the check-in desk waiting to complain

or hear what's next or shout their way out of their current circumstances.

21 • When Frankie and Michael picked the boys up from the motel, Willy and Johnsy and I pushed the fake brass luggage rack across the snowy parking lot to where Michael had parked the car. He and Frankie got out and I hugged them both and we caught up as the flakes fell around us. They'd just flown in from a documentary film premier in LA that Michael had a big role in, and Frankie told me about Alma Richardson, a mutual friend of ours who'd been there. "Michael knew everyone there, but I didn't know anyone, and I was like, *Almaaaa!* I was so happy to see someone I knew." Michael, tall, sad-eyed, with a new beard and a short, stylish ski coat, told me how awful LA was. I told him I thought about LA the same way I thought about Las Vegas. It's great for a day and then you want to get the hell out. As I said it I realized I didn't mean what I was saying, but I kept on for the sake of comradery: "LA is exhausting. LA makes me want to shrivel up and die in a corner like a slug someone poured salt on." Willy and Johnsy hugged me goodbye while Frankie and Michael put their car seats in. Willy cried silently, mopping away the tears with his coat sleeve and then I was crying for the first time since summer a year and a half ago in front of their grandmother's house when Willy wouldn't leave my side for ages he was bawling so hard. When Willy cries I lose it. I can't hold it back. It all flows out of me like a busted dam, the river flooding the valley and destroying all the houses. Johnsy is more resilient. He moves through social situations easier, more confidently. Willy has a tender heart and is hurt often while Johnsy parades through life with a brash, swashbuckling ease. People say everyone loves one of their kids more. Willy and Johnsy aren't my kids, even though they very much are, but

I can't imagine the choice. They're different people. Willy—older, introspective, artistic, melancholic like me, prone to outbursts of emotion, intensely connected to those he loves. Johnsy—a year and a half younger, bold, loud, silly but with an engineer's mind, makes friends easy, lets things roll off his back. They are equally wonderful and so different. To choose one over the other would be a betrayal.

22 • It's nearly dark outside. The blinking lights of the runaway flash gold, green, red—the planes sitting idle in the falling snow. A pop song comes on in the bar. Something tells me it was the #1 song the day Johnsy was born and I look it up on my phone and I'm right. It's funny the things you know about the people you love. I love this song for no other reason than because it was #1 when Johnsy was born. I know Willy's favorite Pokémon card and I love it because it's his favorite. Love isn't mystery. *Lust* is mystery. Love is *knowing*.

23 • I cried in the motel parking lot, but I'm not crying now. I'm thinking of the future—the year ahead and what will come. Where will we go when we're forced off our land? When will I see the boys next? How will those in my orbit weather the months ahead? No one is thriving, but everyone is fighting to get by, pushing and hoping. The year to come will be an election year. Everyone I know will work, love, cope, pay bills, make plans, chase dreams, disbelieve death enough to get out of bed in the morning, shove for that next ascending step. We will hope in the midst of the warzone of life. We will hope because we are senselessly optimistic despite the odds. It's part of the human spirit to believe that things will get better. We are a species of beaten optimists. Every year is shit

and glory, defeat and wild triumphs. So, float me away. Carry me off toward the shore of my dreams. Make the impossible possible. Float me away. Float me away. Float me away.

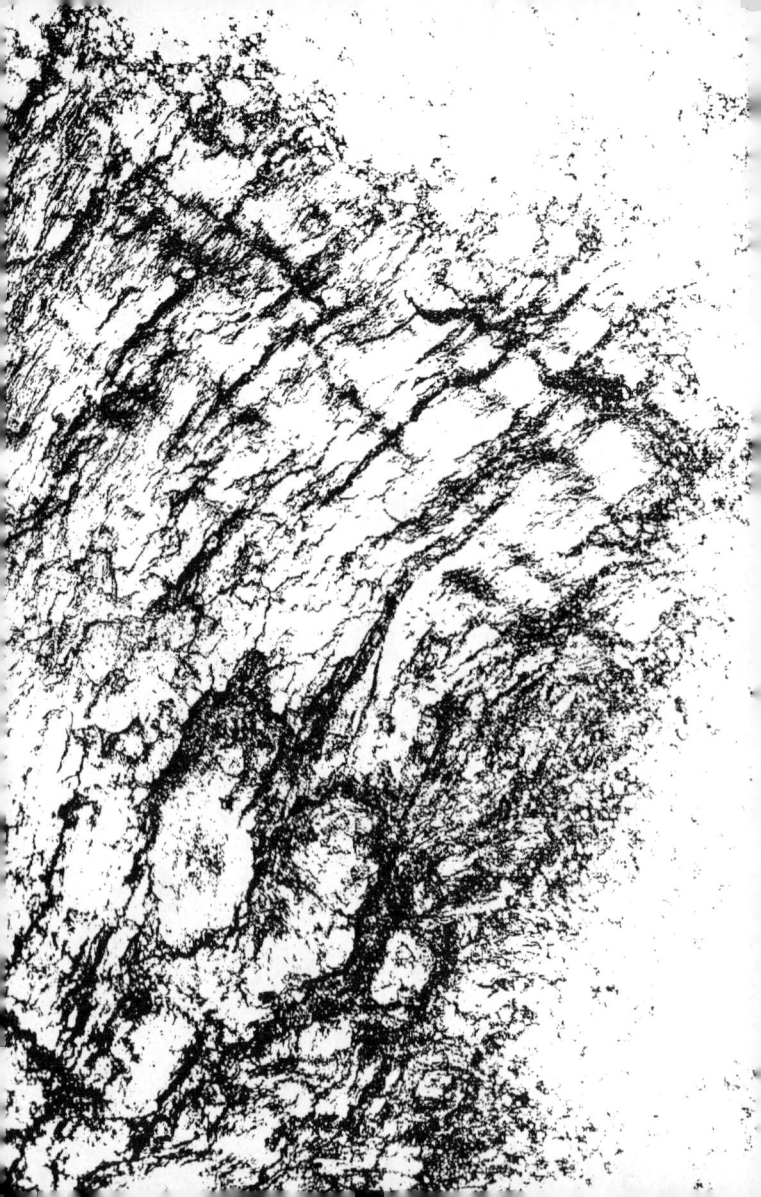

WISH/WANT

This is my invocation. I'm putting it in words and I'm throwing it to the breeze. I'm making a list here and you are the notary and now it's official. I wish to live a good life and at the end of my life I wish to go easy, but I want to know I'm going, and I want to be surrounded by the people I love as I go. I wish to go in a rush of wind that rattles the tree branches then falls silent and still as morning.

WISH

I wish to live a life that's like the relief when you wake up from a nightmare and know it was all just a dream. I wish to wake up rested and with a calm heart. I wish to never be tired when I shouldn't be tired. I wish to think clearly and never stumble over a thought as I struggle to explain myself. I wish to be thought of as eloquent. I wish to say lovely things.

WANT

I want to stand at the fence-line and watch Ward's cattle in the
field moving as slow as ancient time.

WANT

I want to take it slow.

WANT

I want to take my time in this fast, fast life.

WANT

I want to be good, gentle, and true to the people I love, and I want them to think of me as good, gentle, and true.

WANT

I want the people I love to look at me and think: Don't go nowhere.

WANT

I want the sweet ache of our times long past to comfort and
not hurt me.

WISH

I wish to grow old with a straight back and a clear, sharp mind. I wish to grow old with those I love by my side.

INVOCATION

And when my boots have worn out float me away.

INVOCATION

Float me away. When my time here is over.

INVOCATION

Float me away. When my work here is done.

INVOCATION

Let me go nowhere. Let me go.

INVOCATION

Float me away.

INVOCATION

There's a storm rolling in over Weston. Cold rain that will be snow by nightfall. Thunder rumbles in a long, low roll like a distant engine. Icy wind cuts through the skeletons of trees and sweeps across the tawny dead prairie grass, lifting the dry leaves and swirling them upwards, the sky and the farmhouse darkening. There are days ahead and others behind. I wish to live many days past today, the day I sit typing this, New Year's Eve, 10am, still strong, still determined, in the front room of the farmhouse.

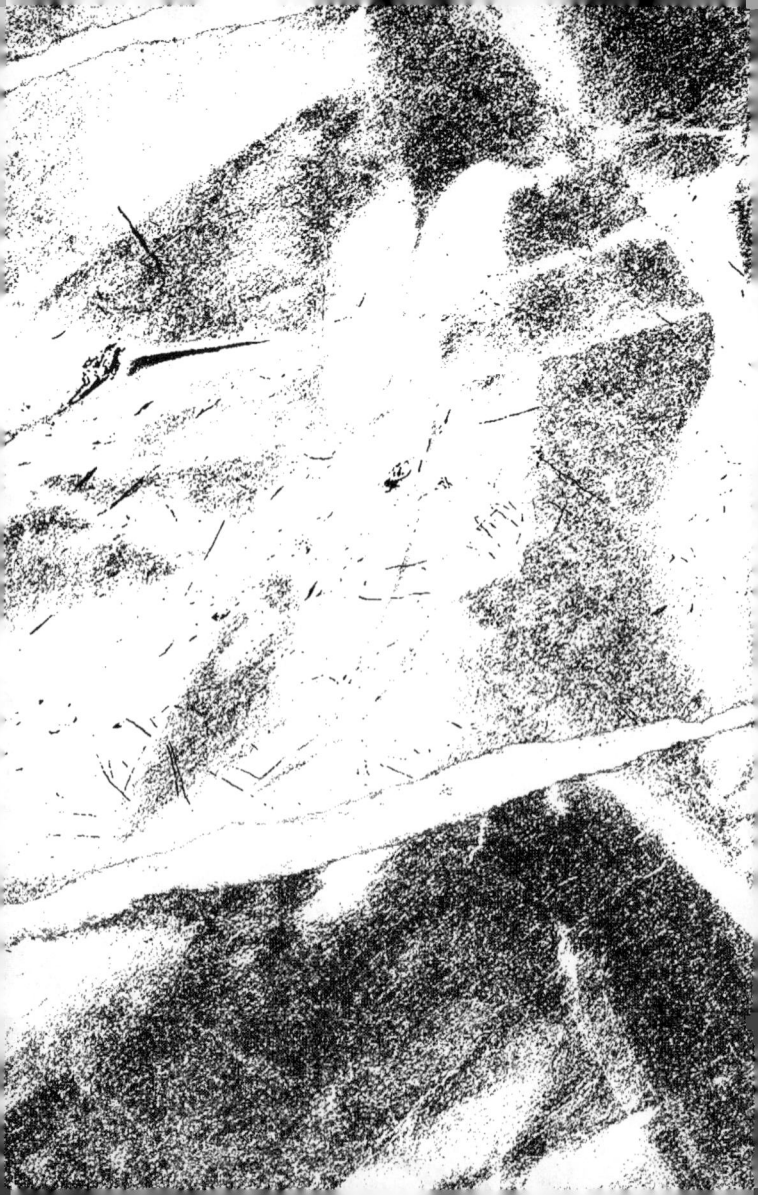

Born in the beach-town of San Diego, California, Adam Gnade has spent the last decade on a farm in the rural Midwest, choosing a reclusive life while continuing to tour the US and abroad behind his releases. He is the author of the novels *Hymn California, Caveworld,* and *This is the End of Something But It's Not the End of You,* the novella *Locust House,* and a solitary work of nonfiction, *The Do-It-Yourself Guide to Fighting the Big Motherfuckin' Sad.* His work is released by Michigan's Bread and Roses Press and San Diego's Three One G as a series of books and audio recordings of writing backed by music that create a shared fictional universe of storylines and characters. His aim is to compile a "fictional, personal history of the United States, telling the story of how it was to live when I lived." He writes, "I plan to leave behind a huge, interconnected body of work that will serve as an inventory of my time on Earth." Inspired by William Faulkner's Yoknapatawpha County, the ongoing collected work is titled *We Live Nowhere and Know No One.*

ACKNOWLEDGEMENTS:

I kept this book top secret while writing it, but a small group of very good people was instrumental in its creation. Huge and endless thanks goes to Rich Baiocco for his good taste and sensibility, Nick Bernal for the kind words and giving it a read early on, Bran Black Moon for designing the book and making it look beautiful, Jonas Cannon for being a first reader, Julia Eff for knowing their shit and being ironclad trustworthy, Dakota Floyd for the soda advice, Rikka De Herrera for the endless and undying support, Erik Henriksen for the advice only a seasoned newspaper editor and massive nerd could give, KC Book Manufacturing for the printing, Jessie Lynn McMains for giving it a read, my Patreon subscribers for keeping food on my table and listening to early audio excerpts, Justin Pearson and Jessie Duke for giving the book a proper home on Three One G and Bread and Roses, Nate Perkins for all your good advice, Reira Rose Moon for the design help, and Bart Schaneman for the edits and rereads. Special thanks goes to Hugo Manuel, Sandy Bull (RIP), Jack Rose (RIP), and Jimmy LaValle's the Album Leaf for the music I listened to while writing this, and Carolyn Forche, Ana Castillo, Ocean Vuong, Jesmyn Ward, and Sandra Cisneros for keeping me inspired with your excellent work. Most of all, eternal thanks goes to Elizabeth Thompson for loving and taking care of me during the year I spent writing this. This book is dedicated to a couple of very good men, Liam and Jack Christian.

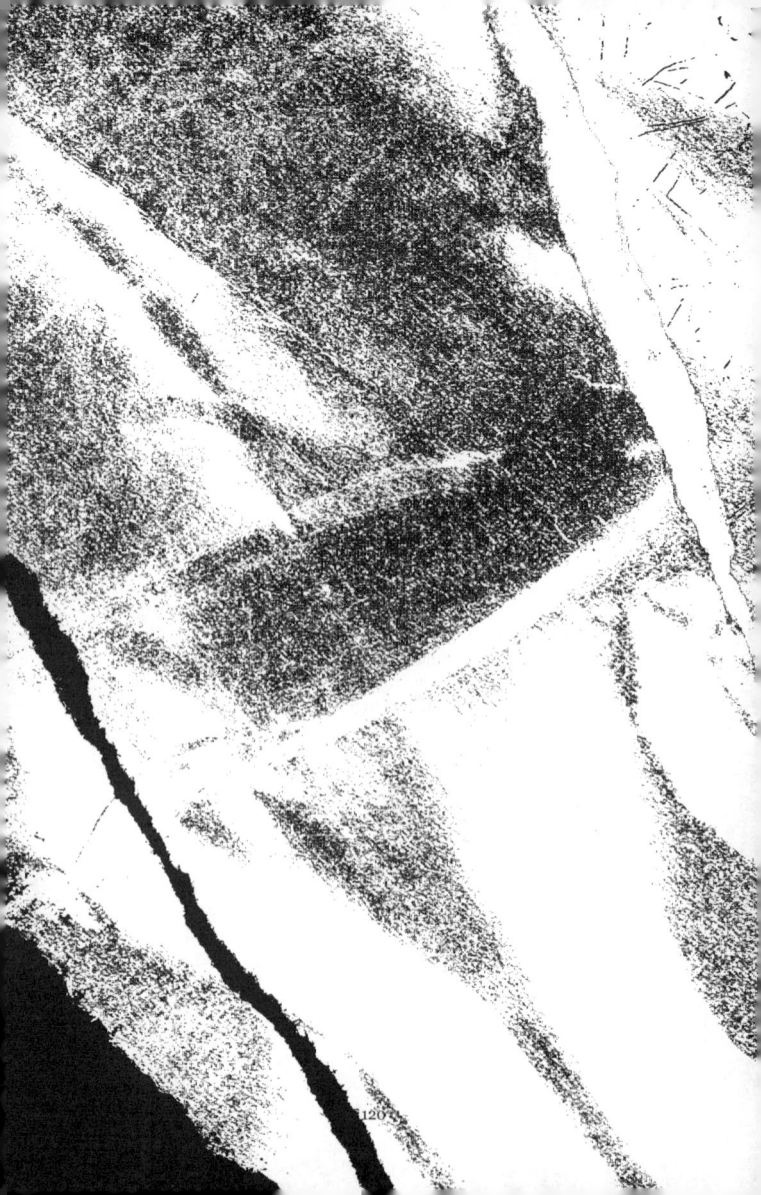